LOVE-FIFTEEN

LOVE - FIFTEEN

by

Antonio Skármeta

Translated by
Jonathan Tittler

Latin American Literary Review Press
Pittsburgh, Pennsylvania
1996

The Latin American Literary Review Press publishes Latin American creative writing under the series title *Discoveries*, and Critical works under the series title *Explorations*.

Library of Congress Cataloging-in-Publication Data

Skármeta, Antonio
    [Match Ball. English]
    Love–fifteen / Antonio Skármeta; translated by Jonathan Tittler.
       p. cm. -- (Series Discoveries)
    ISBN 0-935480-82-X (trade pbk.: alk. paper)
    I. Tittler, Jonathan, 1945–. II. Title. III. Series: Discoveries.
Discoveries.
PQ8098.29.K3M3813   1996
863--dc20   96–4268
                                        CIP

Cover art and design by Valerie Walawender.

Latin American Literary Review Press
121 Edgewood Avenue • Pittsburgh, PA 15218
Tel (412)371-9023 • Fax (412)371-9025

My biography can be summarized in three words: American, Harvard, fucked-up.

I got my medical degree back in a time when I weighed ten pounds less, even with hair that weighed five pounds more. The hippies' erotic effusions and the student protests embellished my youth but left no great imprint. Between the Republicans and the Democrats, I always voted for the Democrats, less out of economic conviction than because of my friendship with Jacqueline Bouvier, the Kennedys, and William Styron.

I let nothing stand between me and my studies, and I was always ready to forego Boston's social pleasures in order to bone up for some exam. It would be hypocritical to say that I was not interested in starting my own practice at once and becoming a prestigious physician replete with fame and fortune.

My Harvard degree, along with my confirmed bachelorhood, my discipline, and my familial and political ties, brought me a reputation of professional excellence, and I would have even come to occupy an endowed chair at my alma mater if I had not had the inspiration one day to attend a cocktail party in honor of some foreign professionals.

That's where I met her. A woman whose aristocratic pedigree glowed like an aura of sainthood. That she was a baroness, a millionaire, cultured, and intelligent I knew before exchanging a word with her. Those years at Harvard nurture a sixth sense for detecting such defects in people—defects for which, I should confess, I have a personal weakness.

Luckily, this woman had a slight flaw. She knew Italian and French, but only a little English. With aristocratic pride, she was not willing to speak a language she did not wield with perfection. That fact led that beautiful woman to exile herself in a shadowy corner to suffer our California chablis. I went over and asked her name. She answered with two utterances. "Ana von Bamberg" and "I speak no English." Noticing her accent, I replied in German, "A virtue I applaud." And upon seeing her generous green eyes shine in that salon, for the first time in my life I forgave my parents for having sent me to Boston's Deutsche Schule.

I despise those who claim they will be brief, and years later their pronouncement continues to prove to be empty rhetoric. I'll skip over luscious stretches of our tale and touch only upon the milestones. Months after the cocktail party I married Ana von Bamberg and came to live in West Berlin, where my father-in-law presented us with a mansion and me with an office appointed with everything modern medicine can offer. Those who had detected in me a talent for social climbing found in my resplendent new position reasons to confirm their suspicions.

If the truth be known, I should confess that an office of those dimensions, adorned with originals by Duffy and David Hockney, would have been far beyond my own means. So the fact that, in that somewhat rustic Germany, I felt no nostalgia for my mundane days in New Hampshire, I owe to my father-in-law. He is also responsible for introducing me to the sport of my perdition: tennis.

"The sport of my perdition." A strange sentence for a doctor, convinced as I am that for the most part my patients' ailments were due to too little exercise and too much food. My growing prestige in Berlin stemmed from placing my patients on a stringent diet, something that, to be sure, even a quack could manage, but with an added detail that was the key to my success: I would encourage those who lost a couple of pounds per week with praise that would have made a schoolboy blush. Nothing impels a German more than efforts rewarded. One example of my technique: If some day I ran into Günter Grass I wouldn't just say to him "I really enjoyed your novel *The Rat*" but rather "It must have taken you years to write *The Rat!*"

My father-in-law was a diehard athlete. A fervent supporter of my therapy, he pointed out that if I kept on indulging in those voluptuous German *kuchen*, soon I would put on so many pounds that my patients would no longer consider me credible. My father-in-law is an absolute delight whose only weakness is a certain tendency to preach in proverbs: "What's good for the goose is good for the gander." Ergo, we decided—he decided—that I would be his singles partner in the tennis matches he played at the exclusive Golf Club. These took place on weekdays between seven and eight in the morning, come rain, fog, snow or sun, and on Saturdays at noon. Baron von Bamberg had not rested on his family's laurels. On the contrary, buoyed by the economic upswing of the German Federal Republic, he invested millions in the chemical industry and managed to double his capital in the last five years. To keep costs down, every time there was an accident in the industrial plants that line the Rhine, the employees saw to it that the toxic residues from the factories were dumped into the formerly romantic river. "A few more dead fish won't harm anyone," he would say with the smile of a naughty child.

Within a brief time the matches with my father-in-law on the groomed courts of the Golf Club ceased to be an arduous fawning—which resounded to the benefit of my bank account—and turned into a pleasure. Those ounces of fat that I combatted so rancorously in my clients disappeared, I began to look younger than my 52 years, and I enjoyed watching the technical progress in my own game. The moment arrived when I knew with certainty I could defeat my seasoned father-in-law in every set, although for obvious reasons I limited myself to winning at a rate of only fifteen percent. I began to read specialized magazines, I bought videos of great matches, and for my birthdays and at Christmas time I suggested they give me rackets, which I collected with the verve of a philatelist. I searched among the leaders of the sports world for those with whom I could identify. Finally I consecrated as my prophet Jimmy Connors: a discrete veteran who seldom won a tournament, someone who was regarded the way one listens to a

melody from one's adolescence—with a patina of happy nostalgia—but who was still sufficiently active to occasionally defeat the
arrogant younger champions. In short, an idol cut to my measure-
ments.

Aside from my solidarity with his age, I myself was
surprised by this predilection toward Connors. I, who grow dizzy
in the presence of vulgarity and emotional outbursts, ought to have
looked for a less strident master. I abhor the obscene gestures and
piquant phrases that charm the sporting press. The loves in his
biography have been equally distinctive. Pleasant his passion for
Chris Evert, too spicy for an originally elegant sport his dalliance
with ex-Miss World Marjorie Wallace , and odious his marriage to
the Playboy model Pat McGuire. I can't keep the order of events
straight. Did Connors interest me at first because of the aggressive-
ness of his style, the legacy of his tutors Pancho Segura and Pancho
Gonzalez, or precisely for his tortuous biography, in which tennis
intermingled with ladies of erotic ambience?   It is not without
apprehension that I ask the question of whether my self-image was
not for decades that of a Freudian superego inflated by the courte-
sans of Harvard, while in my unconscious there struggled the
caricature of a libidinous demon that the press has wanted to make
of me.

*   *   *

Everything in my life was going along swimmingly until
a robust adolescent, with the happy blankness of expression of a
diligent schoolboy, won the great tournament at Wimbledon.
From that moment on, life in Germany was thrown topsy-turvy. At
the slightest provocation parents would grab their children by the
ear and say: "If you try hard, some day you'll go that far." The most
powerful bank in the Republic ran newspaper ads with the boy's
photo and the caption: "The fruits of effort." The godlike triumph
of this child, who probably still celebrates his successes sucking on
lollipops or chugging milkshakes at McDonald's, was indirectly
the cause of my ruin. The courts of the Golf Club teemed with
freckled children—I do not rule out the chance that their idolatry

led some to the extreme of painting on freckles whose texture resembled that of their idol—who by six in the morning would bare in the locker room their unbiased youthful attributes. Tennis, costly to play and long a bastion of the aristocracy, was now a mass phenomenon. The television sportscasts began to dedicate more time to tennis than to soccer. One Monday my father-in-law discovered in his private locker at the club a pair of flowered Bermuda shorts. On Tuesday, after playing a match amidst a thundering din of thousands of neighboring rackets making impact, he fainted in the shower when two adolescents applied a vibrator to their bodies. And on Friday of that same week he met me repentantly at the door of the club. The courts were not available that day owing to a special event "that honors our institution" (according to the sign over the gate). Baron von Bamberg briefed me as he consoled me over coffee at the bar: the courts had been closed to the Golf Club's most conspicuous members because a certain Miss Sophie Mass, number one seed in the stunted Berlin championship, wanted to train unfettered, free of spies, witnesses, admirers, or servile functionaries. About Sophie Mass—Miss Mass—I knew a few things in general: that she was extremely young, scarcely fifteen years old, that she was a gazelle on the court, that her serve, a product of her fragile developing body, was not the strongest, and that she compensated for these frailties by the speed with which she could retrieve a ball from wherever her opponent should wish to place it. She was also celebrated for the millimetric precision with which she could put the ball out of her competitor's reach and for her socialistic refusal to wear commercial logos on her shirt, arguing that business had no right to use sports for its own purposes. I know that this statement had whetted the appetite of numerous large publicity firms, which were aware that such idealistic attitudes suited a rising star and were waiting only for Sophie to win an important tournament before making her an offer that would destabilize her idealism, whether spontaneous or tactical. Besides, I had read an article in *Tennis* magazine by the visionary expert Ulrich Daiser, who predicted that in the next few years there would be two German tennis players who would win both the coveted Wimbledon cup and an Olympic gold medal.

The first name was woefully obvious: a fact even the dumb shouted in the streets. With the second name, however, Daiser risked his reputation for perspicacity: Sophie Mass. Another of my father-in-law's tidbits piqued my curiosity: it could be that through Sophie Mass's veins coursed (these were the Baron's very words) more blue blood than there are pollutants in the Rhine. Proof of her power was right before my eyes: she had closed down all the Golf Club's courts in order to practice at her ease. That the administration had willingly complied to this neurotic impulse, or infantile whim, leaving prominent shareholders in the street, indicated that the little one had a lot going for her. It was plain, added the Baron, that Miss Mass did not issue from an anonymous German village from the bosom of an anonymous family with anonymous surnames and anonymous origins like the anonymous racket wielders who filled the pages of the national press. Rather, she had class, rank, lineage, polish, pedigree (I swear), and she did not take pains to hide it. At this point I began to understand why the normally irascible Baron had meekly accepted the Club's refusal to allow him on the court.

Of the starlet's mother and trainer it was said that she had had an interesting career—without glory—in the sixties. Sure that she herself would never make it to the top of the world rankings, she decided, instead of vegetating in the senior pastures à la Guillermo Vilas, to retire from the courts, issuing a statement that intrigued the aristocrats and to this day is quoted in the romance magazines: "I am giving up tennis because I am expecting a child. In a few months I will give birth to a princess."

The uncertainty of whether Countess von Mass had used the term princess in a metaphorical sense, or if, as a matter of fact, the father was a king, persisted. Palace denizens opined that sporadic and clandestine contacts with a monarch were not out of the realm of probability. For that reason my father-in-law was inclined to take the sobriquette princess literally. The press had a field day with that uncertainty, and speculation about the princess's paternity led to cartoons in which she was attributed with Swedish or Spanish features, with no regard for the Scandinavian social system or for the democratic stability of the Iberian Peninsula in the 1980s.

Doing constant battle with these foes had sharpened Countess von Mass's steel tongue to guillotine keenness. As for her daughter, the princess, it was said she was so delicate and beautiful that if she was not a real princess she was worthy of being one.

*   *   *

You will forgive me if, drunk with curiosity and fortified by my morning cup of coffee, I confronted the Golf Club doorman, bribed him with the promise to treat in my office his acne-riddled daughter, infiltrated the club's familiar contours, and spied from below the grandstand of Maud Watson Stadium on the secret training session between mother and daughter.

The Countess fed balls to the princess with scanty maternal tenderness. Judging from the force of her serve, one could not help but assume she would have had success as a professional, even at her age, which was perhaps a couple of years shy of Jimmy Connors'. But the mother's potential athletic prowess is of no moment to our story. Sophie let one of her serves go by, raised the racket pensively, rested it on her shoulder, and during an instant seemed to be listening to the musical strings of her Prince Graphite.

"Mom," she said, "there's someone on the court."

The Countess held her breath and scanned the entire field. I felt ridiculous about my childish behavior, but my embarrassment paralyzed me.

"There's someone on the court," Sophie repeated, talking to herself.

"Where?"

"I don't know, Mom, but I can feel it."

All of a sudden it seemed that both glances penetrated the stands and focused on my body. I thought I had to respond with some elegance to my ridiculous position. Taking control of my muscles, I gave the ladies a healthy Harvard greeting (relaxed appearance, but alert mental state) and approached them like an absent-minded professor. On the spur of the moment I came up with a couple of compliments in the flowery style of a Latin lover: corny expressions that were tedious enough for the victim to grow bored and to forget her pent-up anger. Having faulted in my first serve, I addressed myself directly to the girl.

"Dear Sophie, please excuse this intruder, this thief of solitude, whose only crime is his admiration for you, tripled now that I see you close up and can confirm that your beauty is as great as your talent."

Sophie listened to my palaver with an ironic half-smile, but it was her mother who replied with the energetic staccato of an Irish actor.

"Your first insolence was to steal into this place like a rat, the second to address a minor before her mother, and the third to call my daughter dear. By your accent and your behavior I assume you are an American, that abominable species that confuses spontaneity with impertinence."

"I beg your forgiveness from the depths of my soul."

"The depths of your soul? Americans have no depth. They are pure surface."

Scratching the tip of my nose, I said to her:

"I would be willing to bet your next sentence will be 'Yankee go home.'"

"Thank you for saving me the trouble. Good-bye." The mother bounced the ball on the ground.

"You, Madame, shoot from the hip."

"I learned it in the films of your compatriot John Wayne."

Ignominiously defeated, I turned to the daughter for help.

"Sophie ..."

"Please cut the crap," said the girl, and she turned deliciously away to walk toward the backcourt.

"*Aufwiedersehen*," I said. This German expression holds something optimistic and intimate that is lacking in *adiós* or in our indifferent good-bye. I was retreating in confusion from below the ignoble grandstand where I had spied on the training session, when I stumbled in my lair upon a pale young man who was looking stupefiedly toward the court. He seemed not to notice my presence. The script I was enacting indicated that I ought to speak to him.

Which, to my regret, I did.

*   *   *

"I see, young man, we share the same vice."

He gestured toward me disdainfully and turned his eyes again toward the court.

"Since long before you."

"An admirer of the tennis star?"

"Admirer? You confuse cancer with the common cold."

"An accusation that, as I am a physician, touches me especially. What is your ailment?"

"Sophie."

"Son, I believe I am going to ask you to do me the honor of accepting a milkshake at McDonald's."

There was such despondency in his expression that I took him by the arm.

"Leave me alone," he told me, on the verge of tears.

"Let's go, my boy, or they'll drag us out of here in handcuffs."

There is a Viennese café on the corner abutting the Golf Club where they serve up some glorious *Bienenstich*. It was there I took the adolescent, who seemed to have lost his powers of speech. When they brought our tea he maniacally stirred the liquid with his teaspoon. After five minutes I struck his cup with a knife to break his trance.

"If you will permit me a parenthesis in this intense dialogue, I wish to inform you that, since I have served you no sugar, there is no reason to stir your tea."

He dropped the utensil on the table and almost fainted back over his chair. From that reclining position he stared disquietingly at me.

"Are you a tennis player?"

"I was a tennis player."

"You gave it up so soon."

"I'm seventeen. But I feel like I've lived a century."

"A little tea. It does worlds of good for melancholy."

He ignored my suggestion. With sudden intimacy he put his elbows on the table, cupped his chin with his hands, and told me, "I live in Madrid, but for the past month I have been following Sophie to every country where there is a tennis tournament."

"I presume, from your pallor, that it is not merely a dedication to the sport that attracts you to her."

"I love her desperately."

"And the beneficiary, is she aware of the illness?"

"I have told her with my look, with my hands, with my silence, with my presence in every city where she has played."

"I fear Sophie takes you for a mute."

The youngster extracted a weak smile from the depths of his sadness.

"I see you are making fun of my illness, Doctor."

"On the contrary, I have extraordinary sympathy for your condition. But the ever-popular aspirin will not suffice to cure it."

The *Bienenstich* arrived, and even before mine was placed on the table I seized it and took a deep bite. Savoring it, I said, "I imagine that moving from city to city must run into some money."

"I use my father's checkbook."

"A very generous progenitor."

"Don't believe it. He's an old miser. What happens is that I have a special talent for forging his signature."

I stood up. "Raymond Papst," my intuition telegraphed me, "the time has arrived for you to take your leave."

"I guess I shouldn't have ordered tea at this time of day."

"Are you afraid?"

"Me, afraid?"

"You invite me to tea, which you have yet to touch, and you are already asking for the bill. Relax. I'll pay for it."

"Oh, no, son. I don't want to be an accomplice to embezzlement."

When I placed the money on the table, the boy took my hand and, with his eyes, begged me to sit down.

"Help me, Doctor."

"How, my boy?"

"Sophie's mother won't let her have any friends. She

wants her to devote herself only to tennis. Please, convince her to let me see her."

"Me! You've already heard the choice words she said to me on the court."

He took a pen from his jacket and on a napkin wrote with feverish hand the number 304.

"Then deliver this message to Sophie. Tell her I'm at the Hotel Kempinski."

"Young man, you are merciless with your father's checking account. The only way I can help you is by recommending a good hotel with only three stars."

I crumpled the napkin in my hand and threw the wad on the table.

"You are responsible for whatever happens to me," the boy said somberly. "You are the only person I know in Berlin. The only person who can help me."

"For that pallor I can give you some vitamins in my office. Here is my address. As for the rest, I can only advise a return flight to Madrid."

The youth took my card.

"'Dr. Raymond Papst,'" he read aloud. I looked around me like a suspect in a criminal lineup. "You'll read about me in the newspapers."

"What are you planning to do?"

"It will be your fault," he said this sentence twice, once in German and another time, to himself, in Spanish.

I grabbed the boy's *Bienenstich*.

"If you're not going to eat your *Kuchen*, I may as well take it with me. I can't resist these pastries."

On the way home I savored the harmonious flavor of the honey and determined to erase from my mind the boy's vague threat. As a physician I have seen with my own eyes how human beings expire from very concrete causes; I was not going to panic over the boast of some snot-nosed kid. I wonder what he wanted to tell me?

Would he try to take his own life? It would be a shame, at such a tender age, but it was something with which I could not involve myself emotionally.

Or was he proposing to kill either Sophie's mother or Sophie herself?

The first possibility—I must confess with a blush—did not faze me. But the second, even just the thought of it, set me atremble. That creature of only fifteen years would within a few months achieve her splendor. That talent and that sensuality were on the earth to bring joy to humanity. She would be an idol. The lives of opaque multitudes—among whom I counted myself— would be enriched by dreams of her beauty and triumph. Why should a pale adolescent, awash in self-concern, be able to put in check a brilliant career with his impertinent complaints?

*   *   *

Baron von Bamberg had taken pains to assemble an unforgettable party. A number of conspicuous bankers, industrialists, close and distant relations, radio and TV managers consumed canapés and liqueurs. On a little dais he had placed a string quartet that interpreted tunes with a Hungarian air. The ladies sported enough jewels for Zsa Zsa to have been in her glory. Even Ana, my wife, had fallen dutifully into formation alongside the Baron to receive the guests. When the controversial Countess von Mass made her entrance, half the world thronged in hope of gathering material for an anthology of gossip. I am inexpert in the art of describing formal attire, but even if destiny had endowed me with said talent, the tension of putting myself on the defensive led me to remember more the words than the jewels or the outfits.

After kissing my father-in-law's cheeks with exaggerated emphasis, the Countess regarded me with the curiosity an entomologist shows for a repugnant insect.

"Countess Diana von Mass. My daughter Ana. My son-in-law, Doctor Papst," said the Baron as his alert pupils darted from one extreme of his eyes to the other.

The Countess congealed her smile and, after moistening her lips, as a swimmer takes air before diving, she said:

"You are a recurrent nightmare, Doctor."

"You, on the other hand, seem to me like a dream."

"Fifteen years ago I would have made the effort to believe you. But tennis ages one faster than alcohol."

My father-in-law, without clearing his throat, spoke as if he had cleared his throat.

"Do you know each other?" And without pausing, she turned her assault on Ana.

"And you, Madame, what do you do?"

"I am a lawyer."

"A very opportune profession. I calculate that sooner or later you will have to get your husband out of jail."

Before she could withdraw, I dared ask her:

"And your daughter is not coming today?"

"She came down with a case of punk rebelliousness. She has ensconced herself in a discotheque with the repugnant name of 'The Dove.'"

Ana and I sighed in unison. The chorus of curiosity seekers took off after the Countess, certain that the evening held great promise. That was the moment when Ana commented, caressing one eyebrow:

"I hope little Sophie hasn't inherited her mother's tongue."

"Oh, no. Sophie has the sweetest tongue on earth."

"How do you know?"

How deceitful are the forests of language. Ana's innocent irony immersed me in an erotic atmosphere that was dissimulated well by the wink with which I celebrated her question. The presentiment of Sophie's tongue slipping softly over my own tongue agitated me. I attribute to that same upset my leaving the party, entering a telephone booth infested with graffiti in order to look for the address of "The Dove," and upon not finding it, setting off to roam the downtown streets. That same upset led me to the main avenue where the dance halls are heaped upon each other and my intuition—or should I say fate—had me descend the stairs of a place called "The Hippopotamus."

I skip over the description of those little torture chambers for adults where one is young in such a brutal way. The music covered the whole range of Lionel Ritchie, one of the few pop artists in whom I recognize a degree of sensuality. Sophie was sitting at a table beside the dance floor. She was staring off at a distant point, and across from her the same suicidal youth I had seen that morning was gesturing dramatically, as if he had three or four hands in front of his face. For a few minutes I took in the magic of the artifice: the large silver ball spun in the middle of the floor and, driven by colored reflectors, showered a carousel of colors on the public. At one moment Sophie was pink, the next she was blue. A crimson turn revealed to me the exquisite texture of her white silk dress, devoid of pleats, adornments, or jewels that might add to its volume. A dress as spare as a bare body. In the distance I could observe that the light fabric rose with her breathing: there was something so insanely fresh in the relation between her body and her clothing.

I advanced toward her like a fifty-two-year-old zombie amidst the swaying and electric adolescents and stopped in front of her table. She did not indicate the slightest surprise. My presence struck her as entirely natural, like the cigarette between the young man's fingers or the champagne on the tablecloth. She smiled at me cordially, and I discovered that in the row of her teeth a certain genteel imperfection, a slight opening in the center, allowed the tip of her tongue to appear.

"How did you know I was here?"

"Your mother spoke of a place with a repugnant name. I guessed it would be 'The Hippopotamus.'"

"I told her 'The Dove.'"

"Only a few kilos stand between a hippo and a dove, darling."

I made the gesture to draw over a seat from the neighboring table, but before completing the motion, I greeted the young man with a nod of my head.

"May I join you?"

The boy looked at me with a stony expression. The syllables shot out like bullets.

"I can't think of a reason in favor."

Sophie gave him a dose of maternal reproach with her glance, and upon seeing that the boy kept leering defiantly at me, she added:

"You don't stand much of a chance for a career in the diplomatic corps, Pablo Braganza."

"Pablo Braganza." The first time I heard his name, which I have never forgotten since. That night of omens, macumbas, intuitions, bravado, everything acquired a relevancy that encircled the trivia the way rust corrodes an object. That night "Pablo Braganza" was just an impertinent lad inspired by the impudence of his scarce years and his father's checkbook, one in a million among the repertory of the tennis star's admirers, maybe swarthier than the average German of his age, perhaps a bit more impulsive because of his Spanish origin, probably better looking, since juvenile acne had not left scars on his livid skin and he possessed a couple of flammiferous black eyes from which the Andalusian factory label seemed to wave. Why then did the mention of his name produce in me a disquieting image?

Braganza paid no attention to Sophie's comment. On the contrary, with an insolence that was worthy of at least a good pull on the ears, he took hold of the fabric of my jacket and, a cynical smile sliding across his lips, he said:

"Look, Doctor, this place is for young people and not for depraved senior citizens."

In hopes of freeing myself from this siege I looked toward Sophie. In a sudden fit of childish informality, she had poured herself over the miniature velvet easy chair, her legs open and extended.

"What are you looking for here?" she said, parading the rim of her wineglass over her lips.

"Defending my dreams," I improvised. "I want to see you win tomorrow and I thought a night of revelry wouldn't suit you."

"I've managed for fifteen years without a father. I don't think this is the moment to adopt one."

Slowly I ran the palm of my hand over the lapel of my jacket, taking refuge in the gesture.

"Do you think I want to be your father? Do I look that old?"

"So old, no, Doctor Papst," Pablito Braganza intervened. "Let's say that the fruit is showing its last radiance before rotting."

A teenager had scored a knockout over me in an improvised verbal exchange. Those years in Boston, my pretensions of
being an alert sort, one who always has his wits on the tip of his
tongue in order to punish pedants and impertinents, were impotent
to relieve my muteness. I was aware of being decentered. A breath
of sanity allowed me to see myself with a bit of objectivity: only
in the bosom of my family could I regain my balance. I was about
to leave the club with a crocodile smile, when Sophie jumped up
from the table and, upon hearing the opening of another of Lionel
Ritchie's sinuous tunes, without waiting for anyone to accompany
her on the dance floor, began to dance with such abandon that her
fragility and lightness were exposed more than ever. Would it be
incomprehensible if I admitted that her beauty caused me pain?

Suddenly Sophie stretched out her arms while keeping
rhythm with the music. She opened them almost ceremonially and
gathered them toward her breast, indicating to me that I should
come dance with her. She held the invitation open with her eyes
fixed on mine, seasoned with the same mischievousness with
which the tip of her tongue had peered out from between her teeth,
without shaking her hair as the other dancers took pains to do, but
rotating the rest of her body as if she were spinning an invisible
hoop about her waist.

Everything spoke in favor of accepting the invitation: my
unconscious, my fascination—which is a good excuse for irrespon-
sibility—and the fact that it was a relatively gentle beat that would
not expose me to ridiculous contortions amidst those supple and
swaying adolescents. Everything spoke in favor of dancing with
her, and yet I did not take the step forward. A last touch of sanity?
Sophie was still there, her arms inviting and welcoming, her hips
full of promise, the silk impregnated with the aroma and temperature of her skin, the blue light of the discotheque that removed her
from reality and evoked in me figures of the first color films of my
infancy.

My hesitation was fatal. A cartoon-like rocker, with a
leather jacket, dark glasses, tousled and greasy hair, smelling of
black tobacco and motorcycle fuel, approached her and took her
humorlessly by the waist. Sophie let herself be tightly enveloped,

resting her cheek on the man's unshaved chin, and they danced in the style that in my youth was called cheek to cheek and whose delights were immortalized by Irving Berlin in a hit that is too ridiculous for anyone to sing today.

I left the discotheque and went out into the winter night, sick with humiliation, frustration, vague nostalgia, weariness.

*   *   *

If in the nocturnal haze Sophie radiated a secret light in harmony with the discotheque's turbid intentions, under the inoffensive Berlin sun and on the hard grass of the Maud Watson Stadium court she seemed like a winged figure. She allowed her opponent's shots to sail over her head, raising her racket more to greet the ball than to hit it. But if one were to confuse this attitude with reluctance, there was soon evidence to the contrary. After a long rally, her opponent found her at the net and cunningly lobbed the ball to the base line. I used the word winged to define my first emotion, and at that instant I understood that it was not a literary expression. In less than two seconds, Sophie Mass was in the exact spot where the ball had bounced. Her rival, a winsome Brazilian name Medrano or Medrado, watched the ball return to her court without managing to budge. She heard the audience's applause with her arms akimbo and the disconsolate attitude with which a soccer goalie regards the ball resting in the depths of his goal.

My father-in-law placed his hand on my knee, and I began to understand that this was the gesture of transcendent moments. He squeezed my kneecap instead of saying to me: What a fantastic kid! And, in fact, Sophie won the first game at love in only forty seconds. Four balls served to the same spot, with the same speed, the same spin, the same joy of playing that brought the crowd to its feet with exclamations of astonishment. After the last ball, the applause was mixed with laughter. It happens that the mechanics of winning the points was so monotonous that it seemed Chaplinesque.

Predictably, Sophie won the next four games, with a bit more effort although no less precision. But in the fifth game, when

Miss Medrano was serving, something in the stands distracted her and she lost the point outright. On the next ball she did not even hint at responding. The spectators took this behavior to be a generous gesture toward her opponent. In truth, no tennis player likes to head for the shower room after a humiliating 0-6 drubbing. Sophie (it was the verdict of the first murmurs) was saving her opponent's honor: she would hand her a consolation game, and in the next two she would deliver the *coup de grâce* so as not to prolong the agony. There was diplomatic applause for the young Brazilian, and the spectators readied themselves for the glorious culmination of the task.

The next game was Sophie's serve, but on her first two attempts the ball buried itself in the net. In the lassitude of her movements I could discern a lack of stamina. Her wonderful little suprarenal glands were not discharging the hormones of victory. She lacked what with so much metaphysical grace the sports commentators call a "killer instinct." Before the next serve Sophie shook her racket before her face, as if fanning herself, made to walk over to the judge to tell him something, and dropped to the court in a faint.

I stood up along with the rest of the audience.

As in the best cliché movies, the referee asked if there was a doctor in the house, and as written in the script I again followed, I made my way dramatically amidst the crowd and asked the assistants to carry the princess to the dressing room.

*   *   *

I extracted a thermometer from my jacket, shook it, and gestured for her to open her mouth. She looked at me and stubbornly pressed her lips shut.

"Come, now. It's only a harmless thermometer."

She opened her mouth slowly, and when I brought the object near her, she bit between her tongue and teeth the finger that held it.

"It seems to me, my little one, that your illness is called anthropophagy."

"Like the cannibals that eat people?"

"Aha!"

"You think I want to devour you?"

I ran my free hand over the bridge of my nose and whispered imprudently:

"For being chewed by those teeth I would gladly trade my father-in-law's fortune."

Sophie smiled, without loosening the pressure on my finger. I looked toward the door, from where echoes of a disturbance reached me. Then the authoritarian voice of my father-in-law demanding silence.

"If your mother comes in now and sees the verve with which you lick my finger she will turn me ipso facto into a cadaver."

The girl released the pressure and I put the thermometer under her tongue.

"Did you drink anything last night?"

"With thith thing in my mouth I can't thpeak."

"That doesn't matter. What did you drink?"

"Champagne."

"With daddy's check!"

"What?"

"And after the discotheque, what did you do?"

"I went to thleep."

I took out the thermometer, and while I lifted it to read her temperature, she replaced it with the tip of her pinky. That gesture inspired in me the following question:

"Alone?"

"Alone?"

"I'm asking if you went to sleep alone."

"You're jealous, Raymond Papst!"

"Sophie Mass: my professional services have concluded. I prescribe for you an aspirin."

I made to get up. She instantly erased the smile from her face, and a new adult expression emerged from her features. Her photos in the papers always falsify her naturalness. I should report that close up her honey-colored eyes convey a look tinged with something secret, indefinable for a man clumsy with words. I know that I speak the truth and lie at the same time if I say that look had something sexual about it.

"Help me, Raymond."

"With what?"

"Last night I didn't sleep in my hotel."

"Where, then?"

"At the Kempinski."

I riveted my glance on the red point of the thermometer and felt the muscles of my face harden. There was Sophie Mass twirling and twisting in the discotheque and above her flowing chestnut hair, the great silver ball was turning and bombarding her with unreal lights, and she opened her arms and invited me to dance.

"The Kempinski," I managed to repeat, after a while.

The girl dug her nails into the shoulderpads of my jacket.

"Pablo told me that if I didn't go with him to the hotel, he would commit suicide."

I removed her to arm's length and, with my hands on her shoulders, said with a didactic little tone that hid my anger perfectly:

"Dearie, that is an old trick of a desperate lover. Only with an innocent creature like you could it have succeeded."

"He wasn't acting, Raymond! When I tried to leave for the court he had a revolver in one hand and a bottle of pills in the other. He told me I would be responsible for what might happen if I didn't go back this afternoon."

"I think I've heard that line before. So you didn't sleep last night?"

Sophie gravely shook her head no, but upon reading my assumptions a lightning flash of mischief changed her expression. She could be fifteen, thirteen, or twenty years old. She could lie or be bitingly serious.

"You didn't sleep even a little?"

"No," she smiled, or insinuated, or wounded, or provoked, or invited, or jested, or begged me.

"That explains the fainting spell. You can't play a professional tennis match without having slept the night before."

"What should we do?"

She said it like that, in the plural. There was something we had to resolve in common. Just like that. Serious, definitive.

"My advice goes against science. What you ought to do is go take a siesta, but it would be a tragedy for my father-in-law if his idol lost by a forfeit. Besides, my reputation as a miracle-working physician would be ruined. Ergo, you return to the court, win the two games you need, and later you can nod off to sleepyland."

"And you?"

"I'll hear of your triumph on the radio and listen to the interview with the winner, probably in jail."

"Raymond," she said to me with a transcendent expression, "thanks."

*   *   *

I got into the car with a level of energy worthy of a better cause. Who had told me to get involved in messes that were none of my concern, and why did I do it with something resembling enthusiasm? Nothing that had happened with Sophie and her family indicated that I should play the good samaritan. Her mother, and the astute suitor, had exposed me to ridicule every time chance or my own clumsiness had us cross paths. As for Sophie herself, I had the impression she was playing cat and mouse with me. But the friendship with a rising starlet flattered me, and I felt a paternal tenderness toward a girl subjected to the high tensions of professional tennis. My advice of the night before in the discotheque had deserved a cutting rejection from her: she did not need a father. Now, of course, she was paying the price for her haughtiness.

I burst into room 304 of the Kempinski in true detective-movie style. Pablo Braganza, electrified, leaped out of bed.

"Okay, my boy," I said, "I've come to help you pack."

"Out of here!" he shouted.

I went toward the bedside table, grabbed the vial of tablets, and poured the contents over the bed.

"So these are the famous suicidal tablets. How many did you take?"

"I don't plan on telling you!"

"Any court in the civilized world, including a German one, would find you guilty of forgery and bribery! Give me your father's number in Madrid."

The boy lunged for the phone and covered it with a hand. He looked at me with a helpless expression.

"My only crime is falling in love, Doctor."

"With that line you may be able to compose a hit song, but you can't ruin Sophie's life. Pack your bag!"

"The only way I'm leaving Berlin is with Sophie!"

I grabbed him brutally by the shirt and shook him without letting myself be moved by his fear.

"Listen up, you little shit! I'm not going to take pity on you. Sophie fainted on the court because you threatened suicide, and to make her think you had gone through with it you didn't show up at the stadium."

"If you don't leave at once I'm going to swallow the whole bottle right now."

"My years of practice enable me to tell you that in that flask there is nothing but aspirin. If you take them all you'll come down with a case of acid indigestion that will rot your youthful bile."

"There are other ways to deal with the problem."

I snapped my finger like a gypsy playing castanets, and then I demonstratively patted the undefined mass in my jacket pocket.

"If you're referring to your revolver, I have it in here."

"That's robbery."

I removed a pair of shirts from the closet and placed them maternally into the fine leather suitcase.

"The police will be more interested in knowing where you got the revolver than in who stole it from you." Seeing him still unwilling, since he had gone to the bag and furiously dumped its contents onto the rug, I applied another dose of my frontal therapy: "And, by the way, so will your father be interested in knowing."

I dialed information.

"'Braganza,' Madrid, right?"

The boy strode slowly over to me, calmly pressed the disconnect button, took the contraption from my hand, and returned it to its place. Throwing himself onto the bed, he said: "When I confessed my worries to you, I never thought you would be an informer."

That docile attitude struck me as nicer. I detest people incapable of facing up to the truth and who insist maniacally, beyond what patience can tolerate, on their strident behavior. Pablo, sad, serene, in control of himself, seemed as pleasant as when we had co-spied the practice session at the Golf Club. I sat down beside him and said in an affectionate professional tone:

"Let's do without the stalling. Instead, I'll take you to the airport, you make out one of your famous little checks to Iberia, and tonight in a Madrid pub you meditate with absolute calm on how your life is going."

"And Sophie?"

"Sophie plays this weekend in France."

We got up and loaded his things into the suitcase again, I with haste and he with the speed of a striking laborer. While replacing the death pills in the vial, I tasted one of them with the tip of my tongue. Unbeatable with pills, Raymond Papst: the classic taste of acetylsalicylic acid. As he rolled up a pair of well traveled socks, the young man asked almost hopelessly:

"Did Sophie say anything about me?"

"That you are a delightful lad, that she has immeasurable affection for you, that you are one of the few Spaniards with the manners of a courtesan, but that she is still very young for a steady relationship."

He listened to me with so ingenuous an interest, and he made so affable a gesture upon placing his arm on my shoulder, that I felt we had been pals our whole lives.

"I would be happy if I could maintain even a sporadic relationship with her. I know I have a lot to give her, I know that loving her brings out the best in me."

"I'm not sure whether that narcissistic utterance necessarily confirms that you love her. When one is in love he lives for the other, he desires success and happiness for the loved one, he doesn't place roadblocks in her way."

The boy removed his hand from my shoulder. He brought it to his other hand, interlocked his fingers, and cracked them hard.

"You don't have a high opinion of me, do you, Doctor?"

"The best in the world. But I can't refrain from telling you what experience has taught me."

He slowly ran the tip of his tongue over his lips, moistening them. They were fleshy, well delineated. Fallen and beaten as he was, he was immensely beautiful.

"Let's go," he said somberly.

For obvious reasons, I did not want to watch while he paid the hotel bill. I kept at a distance, but not so great that I couldn't cut him off if he opted for another route. I noticed, nonetheless, that a woman at the reception desk was observing Pablo with interest. In a moment the youngster picked up on the glance, and the woman smiled, tossing her hair back voluptuously. Pablo smiled at her and the woman returned his smile. Then he came toward me balancing the suitcase with a carefree air.

In the car he uttered not a word. I drove slowly, trying not to pay attention to the city's depressing architecture. It reminded me of the Far West, where each person made camp helter-skelter, without consideration for the rules of urbanization. To relieve the tension I turned on the radio and tuned into a station that was playing chamber music. With his fingertips, Pablo began to tap out the rhythm on his thigh.

Before presenting his passport at the airport police booth, he turned toward me:

"Doctor Papst, this story does not simply end here."

And with a vulgar gesture that plunged me into a sea of contradictions (I hope you will excuse the crudeness of the verb), he grabbed his sexual member and rubbed it masturbatorily.

"What do you think Sophie and I did last night? Hold hands?" he said, almost chewing the words.

"I don't care to know," I responded, red with wrath and shame, sullied by his vulgarity, on the verge of striking him.

We turned our backs on each other simultaneously, he toward his Boeing, I toward the car. I knew I could not drive without putting in danger both my life and that of the pedestrians. I sat speechless with the car keys in my hand, squeezing them until they hurt me. I was cooking with rage. Who, dear God, had put me up to getting involved in this adolescent conflict?

I returned to the airport bar and quaffed a whiskey with lots of ice. While gamboling with an ice cube on my flaming tongue, I took stock of the situation. Mission accomplished. Sophie had won her match and my father-in-law could boast of his son-in-law's professional services. By now, Countess von Mass probably had forgiven my impertinence of the first day and would have the juicy tournament check tucked in her mother-of-pearl handbag. The youthful nuisance was in flight toward his father in Madrid, accommodating the explicit request of the daughter and the tacit one, I imagined, of the mother.

Everything in order. Period.

*   *   *

God's mercy is infinite: after Sunday, the week began with a glorious Monday in which batallions of moribund old ladies converged on my office, followed by children with broken femurs or tonsilitis with purulent streptococci, and, like the droplet that overflows the pitcher, a Pakistani couple sent urgently by my wife, Ana. In this case it was not a matter of curing their illness, but of inventing one. I believe I've mentioned that Ana is the only extravagance in the Bamberg family. Instead of attending to large corporations and consortia, Ana maintained a law practice worthy of a missionary: she arranged political asylum for Africans, Arabs, Poles, Chileans, and the day there is a dictatorship on Mars, she will get a residence permit in Berlin for the Martians. It's her way of getting even with her family. I doubt that Baron von Bamberg collaborated with the Nazis, but I'm not convinced that he worked against them either. I imagine he celebrated Hitler's defeat by uncorking a bottle of champagne, but I cannot conceive of his hiding a Jew in his mansion, as did a few aristocrats for whom

Hitler was an indigestible dish. There were so many Germans in exile that once democracy was reestablished, everybody's humanitarian vocation was awakened and they passed laws that would make this country the exiles' promised land.

But one thing is the spirit and another, the letter. After years of unemployment, the exile law turns out to be more generous than the officials who find themselves cornered by the laid-off workers, and the government has created an army of legal eagles who ignominiously challenge the foreigners' right to be recognized as exiles, sometimes driving them to suicide. When the poor candidates—who have no money, no language, no contacts, and only the instinct to survive—are declared fit to return without risk to the dictatorships from which they came, they are assigned to a room called the "deportation parlor." The only way to get them out is by using stalling tricks, lest they be placed on a plane within forty-eight hours. One of these tricks is to certify that the clients are so gravely ill that it would be a crime against humanity—Ana writes in her petitions the word HUMANITY in capitals in order to strike the precise moral hammer blow to the head of the police officer on duty—to oblige them to travel . . . And who is the professional samaritan who supplies these certificates of ill health to such a select clientele? Doctor Raymond Papst!

The day they discover the number of cases of Lebanese appendicitis I have collected in my notebook, Chilean pre-infarctions, Ethiopian kidney stones, Thai internal hemorrhages, and Salvadoran hepatitis, they are going to revoke my license and issue me instead the title of Professor Doctor of Infinite Assholery.

And to inaugurate this week—which I would have liked to tear from the calendar—Ana von Bamberg Papst sent me a little note in English, using the nice formula with which she described her candidates for the guillotine: "Darling, please find attached to this page the couple Mr. and Mrs. Salam who are both extremely ill. Love, A." Now they stood before me, alert, silent, sweet, terrified, and I had to think up a plausible illness for them to share equally, while my secretary passed calls to me conveying the Hit Parade of attacks of my elderly patients who every Monday without fail confused gases produced by their Sunday sauerbraten with heart failure. I asked both of them their birth dates and, having completed this rigorous physical exam, I gave each one of them a certificate that was sufficiently dramatic to keep them from being expelled and sufficiently vague for me to avoid being convicted: "Mr. and Mrs. Salam cannot travel on the proposed date because of a rampant viral infection." I always add rampant in order to emphasize something that strikes me as too short or weakly formulated.

As soon as the Pakistanis left, contorting themselves in rituals of gratitude and joyous at having contracted the virus that would keep them on the brink of death, my secretary Gaby announced by telephone that she would send the next patient in. The next patient was Sophie Mass. After delicately closing the office door she stood at a distance so I could appreciate her new look: blouse and skirt of black silk, bare feet, and high-heeled shoes in her left hand, hair falling freely over her right cheekbone, and in the midst of her pallor, like a festival of fireworks (begging pardon for this monstrous metaphor) her mouth anointed with a lipstick that seemed to scream: Kiss me! The radical switch in color, after seeing her levitate in white on the stadium courts, ought to have given me a clue as to her multifacetism that would have been useful to help me face the future: today she was a young lady exercising her radiancy with such sovereign elegance that she allowed herself the savage touch of bare feet, conscious that this breach of etiquette made her paradoxically nobler still.

I made a sour face, fiddled with the tops of my patients' clinical files, and spoke dryly and fast:

"My dear champion, I have an army of moribund old ladies waiting outside. How can I help you?"

"I'm sick."

"There are two thousand five hundred other doctors in Berlin. Besides, your illness is cured. The tumor has been removed and it flew last night to Madrid."

Sophie dropped her shoes on the carpet and immediately put both hands behind her neck, slowly lifted her hairdo, and then let it flow down over her forehead and left cheek.

"That tumor has been removed. The other one hasn't."

"My God! Another admirer?"

"I have the sensation that I could faint again at any moment."

"There is no basis for that to happen. The fainting spell occurred because you played tennis in a state of exhaustion."

"I know, but when I walk down the street sometimes I have to hold onto the trees because I feel light-headed."

"That's a form of neurosis. A slight collapse syndrome that any psychiatrist can cure you of with a couple of sermons."

At that moment Sophie opened the buttons of her blouse, and with a speed and suppleness that were impossible to prevent, she removed it and put it neatly on my desk.

"I have confidence only in you," she said. "I want you to examine me."

My colleagues know that in these cases we apply the fervent rule of neutrality. In every doctor-patient relationship there is a deep emotional turbulence. Roles are rapidly established, and we doctors have neither the time nor the inclination to explain to ourselves why this happens: sometimes the patient is the daughter, or the mother, or the sister, or the doctor is the father, or the uncle, or the soulmate. I knew that my agitated soul would battle to establish itself in some of those roles that would allow me to indifferently contemplate Sophie's breasts, as well as all the warm and resilient skin in their environs. But I could not gain any distance. I observed the discreet volume of her breasts with the same profound emotion as if I were caressing them.

"It's not necessary for you to undress," I said in a dry voice.

"Why not?"

"Dear champion, thus far we have had the good fortune to avoid having a corpse in this story, but the way things are going your mother will see to it that I assume that melancholy role."

"My mother agrees with me."

"Agrees about what?"

"That you should be my doctor for the tournament in Paris."

"Thanks, but no thanks."

"The prize is handsome, and I can pay you a good honorarium."

"I don't need the money."

"But I can't risk suffering another fainting spell in the midst of a match."

"There won't be another fainting spell."

She picked up her black blouse calmly, flipped it over her shoulder with a sporting flair, and waited patiently for me to divert my glance from the papers, which I was pretending to scan, and look toward her. When I did, she told me coldly:

"If you don't come to Paris with me, there will be a corpse in this story. But it won't be yours."

"Ah! I see that the preachings of the guru Pablo Braganza have taken hold."

"With the difference that I keep my word."

I stood up and went over to her. I took her blouse from her shoulder and gestured that she allow me to put it on her. She opened her arms to facilitate the movement and I could not help but evoke the moment at the discotheque in which she beckoned to me by gyrating her hips, offering her whole body. I fastened her buttons and avoided meeting her eyes while I spoke to her.

"Perhaps in your fifteen years you have not come across a little word that defines exactly what you are doing: blackmail."

She made a curious motion with her index finger, bringing it almost to the point of my nose, and for a moment I thought she would slide her finger over it. Realizing perhaps that it would be an insolent gesture, she returned the finger to her own nose, scratched it with one fingertip, and said very seriously:

"No, silly. It's not blackmail. It's something else— something I feel and I find it strange that with all your sensitivity you don't realize."

Slowly I raised my glance toward her eyes and kept it there with the same seriousness as she. Then I saw that something else that she felt, or I saw the *mise-en-scène* of that something else she said she felt. If thesis two, *chapeau, madame*, great performance. If thesis one, all the more reason to gulp the saliva that had been accumulating in my mouth.

I closed my eyes:

"First of all, I don't realize anything. Second, even if I did realize I'd prefer not to realize. And third, even if I preferred to realize I shouldn't realize." I opened my eyes, only to see on her scarlet lips an ironic smirk. "Your visit to Berlin has been a parenthesis in my life. I aspire to no more."

"Me a parenthesis?"

"Written in gold, but a parenthesis none the less. The waiting room is full of patients. Good-bye, Sophie."

Without answering and without leaving, she dabbed her pinky in the layer of lipstick of her lower lip and bent it forward with a pensive gesture. Then she seemed to make a decision and her movements sped up. From her purse she extracted an envelope and extended it to me with military haste. I contemplated it, giving it no importance:

"I don't accept payment."

"In this envelope there is no honorarium, Raymond."

"What, then?"

"Your plane ticket. The flight to Paris is tomorrow at six in the evening."

*   *   *

And turning away, she waved bye-bye over her shoulder with her fingers. I opened the package, which seemed too bulky to contain an airline ticket alone. Indeed, beneath the Air France documents lay a book in German whose white cover bore only two words in bold black: *Poems* and *Milosz*. I opened its first page so clumsily that the ticket fell to the floor. There was a dedication written in large letters that filled the whole first page: *For Doctor Raymond Papst, Yours, Sophie Mass.* As you can see, nothing terribly exciting. But at the very edge of the page, in a handwriting that was, rather than minuscule, infinitely tiny, there was something resembling a written line. Placing the probable text under the halogen lamp, I squinted myopically and tried to make out the letters. Sophie had written: *See page 102.* Which I did without a second's delay. There I found a poem which I transcribe below in its entirety:

THE SEA

Hail, oh beautiful Tetis, mother of destinies!
It is not to console myself or cry for my dead
That I return to your bank, my forehead crowned with
flowers.
Nothing will I say of the swift years
That fled with the wind from me at full sail.
Like your abysses, my eyes are serene,
Free now of the sterile charge
Of slowly scanning the shadowed horizon
In search of those miraculous isles
Where love and mirth are, like here, mortal.
Upon leaving us life shows us who we are:
Evening falls, Tetis, in the sky of my day.
I lost my youth: it is gone forever.
I am too old now for the daughters of men;
They cannot understand my love.
So great is it that no being would dare
Accept or nurture it.
For that one needs all of hope and the entire future,
Everything that laughs and cries, deep nature,
Swollen-breasted mother who cannot die.
Blissful is he who submits to human fondness
And from the world receives what he has given.
I sowed the golden seed and did not pick the fruits,
But I save in my soul, indulgent and arrogant,
The consolation of having everything forgiven.
So I dare love the loveliest one of all,
She who, under the yoke of ceaseless labor,
Harbors all of life in her tremulous lap,
Opening its vast ways to men's adventure.
I wish only that her holy abysses
Be pure, free of the haze that envelopes the summer
horizons,
And that across the oceans' entire breadth and length,

Feeding on the ample pleats of my foamy shroud,
An errant bird eats to its content the heart of my love.

I took a deep breath and ran my fingers over my eyelids, as if trying to dispel a hallucination. The poem took my breath away. In this regard men of 50 resemble those of 15; they are both of ages in which words are taken seriously. Until most men reach fifty, with its subtle death warnings, a check is more important to them than a poem.

This poetry confronted me right where it should, in my office, and wrenched me from my professional routine to pose me nothing less than the little question adolescents are wont to ask themselves in bars after downing a bottle of beer: What is life? Raymond Papst, this cannot be life! Could it be possible that to the question "Who am I?" I should answer with my title: "a physician?" And Ana, despite all the admiration her social mystique held for me, was "a lawyer." At the points of contact between our careers we exchanged a few kisses, had a few drinks together, and consumed a symphony or two. But we had ceased being awestruck by the spectacle of existence, and this poem, bestowed safely in my office, seemed like a drop of real blood amidst the mounds of clinical file cards about lives that were as monotonous as my own, those sad yellow cards on which I did nothing more than register death's great advances and small retreats. How I wished the beautiful Tetis would invade with a wave as immense as a cathedral of foam and wash me away, dissolving me in her mortal waters and giving me the sensation of belonging to her and her unfathomable abysses!

                    *   *   *

I headed for the waiting room and, with a remorseful look, confronted the masses: a virus is sweeping across Europe, and not even we doctors are immune to its dire effects. I was not in any shape to treat them since all my scientific knowledge was stewing in a fever that called for immediate rest. There was a din of solidarity. Nothing arouses a patient's emotions so much as seeing his doctor downfallen. Having resolved this matter I invaded Mollenhauer's office, and in a fit of spontaneity I lay the cards on the table, the poem included. After ten minutes my colleague gave his verdict, of which I remember the following pearls: "Any man in this mediocre and confused world would give his eye teeth to have for his wife an angel like Ana, who bore more virtues than a Latin American general had medals: her refinement, her idealistic commitment to her profession in a time of pharisaism, her physical beauty, her noble vision that allowed her to distinguish the wheat from the chaff and to cultivate friendships with people of true value, her network of relationships that cut across diverse social strata, and—I implored him not to say 'last but not least'—her fortune." He adorned this epilogue with a gesture that encompassed not only the office, but all of Berlin and the world. Then he grasped the book with the expression of one whose duty it was to deal with a repugnant insect, and he issued his non-verdict: of this foolishness I do not understand an iota. I took off my tie and, as if at a funeral, repeatedly caressed it between my fingers. When, trying to make a virtue of necessity, I asked him to take over my practice beginning tomorrow, he tossed his head back in a Dantesque gesture and said solemnly: No.

"So, no?" I asked, feigning ingenuousness.

Mollenhauer bit his pinky fingernail and—looking at me condescendingly—issued a rotund "no."

"I'm sorry, Raymond."

I left his office and went to my own, the book moist between my hands. I sank down in the stuffed leather easy chair, incapable of dispelling my confusion. Among a panoply of doubts, the greatest stood out. What sort of incongruency was it that a girl of fifteen, tennis-court princess though she might be, was trafficking verses of that calibre? One would expect her poetic repertoire to consist of clumsy metaphors from the hit parade of popular tunes. Highly suspect, Watson! Adept in sports, letters, and ... Stop! Too unreal a heroine. Of course tennis players lead a life that is not congenial with this baseness we call reality: changes of country at dizzying speed, varied hotels swarming with all sorts of people, disproportionate earnings that separate them from other kids of their age used to dickering with their miserable parents over their Saturday allowance, and, in short, all the glamour, glory, levity, arrogance of their aristocratic affiliations.

Perhaps between one match and another little Sophie read clandestine books under the sheets of de deluxe hotels while her mother attended the nobility's cocktail parties in celebration of her explosive economic career. A utopian thought! In this decade, books are read by the great adventurers of the soul, those who resist the attacks of a mediocre reality and refuse to despair of finding beauty in literature and life. The people who still read books have in their gaze a brilliance that distinguishes them from the multitudes; their readings are almost like that luminous aura good Catholics draw around saints, confusing them with carnival figures, the same believers who represent paradise in their engravings in the form of a zoo. And in spite of my apprehensions, couldn't it be said that Sophie's sensuality was cut, forged in an internal fire that gave her skin *a touch of intimacy*, which was, forgive me this metaphoric slap, an intimate body, and that this made her a unique being and, why not say it, a heroine? Or was I just as jaded as the rest of postwar Europe, convinced that a fifteen-year-old girl who read poetry was unreal or at least anomalous?

The fever I had faked was becoming real. I took the intercom and shouted to the stupefied Gaby to cancel all my appointments for the rest of the week, since I had to travel urgently to the Institute for Tropical Diseases in Paris to seek counsel for the treatment of Dayler's industrial syndrome. On top of that order I gave her another that must have mired her in utter confusion: to swing by the dry cleaner to pick up my tuxedo.

*   *   *

In the airport I had to proceed with caution. Sophie and her mother were surrounded by fans and journalists, and I didn't want to appear by chance in such conspicuous company the next day in the newspapers. I waited until both of them had entered the departure lounge before presenting my passport to the police.

Before passing through the metal-detection device I was on the verge of fainting. The reason for my fright was not just the *ad hoc* image of Pablo's macho gesture. Where was the revolver I had so determinedly purloined from him in the hotel? I felt my jacket pocket and remembered with relief that on Sunday I had worn a linen sports outfit that I put into the suitcase already checked with Air France. That's where the weapon, which in my giddiness I forgot to toss in some sewer, must have been. Just when the guard, with a routine smile, was feeling the keys in my pocket and excusing himself affably for his obligatory impertinence, I asked myself what would happen if the large pieces of luggage were passed through such machinery. A cold sweat beaded on my forehead. Over the loudspeakers my name would be announced and a squad of agents would burst into the lounge to arrest me. What a first-rate scandal in front of Sophie and the Countess! And what an impoverished state of mind in order to confront with naturalness the impending dialogues against the two tennis players, who, to be sure, would oblige me to enter a verbal fencing match of a very different stripe! How was I going to explain the presence of the revolver to the guards? A friendly instrument for hunting quail? Ridiculous!

In the departure lounge, the Countess was the first to notice me.

"Doctor, you are an angel," she shouted, bestowing two sonorous kisses on my cheeks.

"From recurrent nightmare to angel. I've made progress, Madame."

"Let's dispense with the madame, which has me decomposing before my time. You can call me Diana from now on."

Sophie came over toward us. She was carrying in her hands a tennis racket and an issue of *Town and Country*, where they publish articles of immoderate praise about the international nobility.

"So you came," she said in a tone that seemed to indicate indifference as to whether I had come or not.

"I came," I said in a tone that said why not.

"I'm glad," she said in a tone that said probably not.

"A couple of days in Paris can't harm anyone," I said peevishly.

Still standing, she began to flip through the thick, glossy magazine, ignoring me so completely that it dawned on me this trip was undertaken without clear objectives and with confused motives. The princess rolled up the magazine and stabbed me with it in the belly. She said:

"So?"

"So what?"

"Did you read the poem?"

"Yes."

"And what are you going to do?"

"I don't understand."

"What (pause) are (pause) you (pause) going (pause) to (pause) do?"

"What do you suggest?"

"Proceed."

Everything indicated that this playful dialogue would end with a chuckle or at least a smile. The latter is what had crossed my lips when I was stopped by the seriousness with which the girl—compulsive, sad, and beautiful—looked long into my eyes. She was wearing a suit with vaguely Scottish checks whose cut evoked the figure of an equestrian. With her black velvet jockey's cap she had lost a few years. She looked so young this morning that I had the impression that in her lived many women. The one who had taken her body today was only thirteen.

"Raymond Papst?"

"Sophie Mass?"

"Tit for tat?"

"I don't get it."

"I'm waiting for you to give me a poem now."

"Where should I get it, my precious? In airport kiosks they sell only magazines for idiots."

"Make one up. The flight to Paris lasts two hours."

And she walked toward the picture windows to watch the preparations being made on the Boeing 727. My muse was demanding! Not only did I have to attend to her as a doctor, accept her insinuations without reply, regardless of the semantic charge they might carry, and clear her path of suicidals, but I also had to compete with Milosz in the use of the lyre and the pen. "Oh, what a price I have to pay for loving you." Fats Domino.

My tardiness in arriving at the Air France counter had caused them to seat me, separated from the mother and daughter, in the last row, where the turbines spit fire and where the nervous passengers congregate to smoke with such vehemence that it seems they lack the hands with which to grasp their cigarettes.

In order to calm my nerves and my conscience I reasoned in the following way: "Sophie indeed suffered a swoon. In order to continue with her triumphant tennis career, she indeed needed a doctor. Her mother indeed approved of and desired my trip with them to Paris. There was indeed between Sophie Mass and Raymond Papst nothing more than flirtation on her part and incipient madness on mine. Indeed: nothing serious.

*   *   *

The limousine was just the first of the exquisite attentions the Parisian tournament accorded us. In everything one could note the elegant and enterprising hand of Monsieur Chatrier, an athlete of some standing from the early fifties who, after being the captain of the French Davis Cup team for a few years, founded the magazine *Tennis de France*, launching in his editorials such violent criticisms against the moribund International Tennis Federation that the latter, convinced of the motto "You always hurt the one you love," named him its president in 1982. In that decade, with France destitute of tennis greats who could move the masses as the Musketeers—Borota, Cochet, Lacoste and Brugnon—had done in the 20's and 30's, winning the French International Championship nine times in a row and on six successive occasions capturing the Davis Cup, the dynamic Monsieur Chatrier raised funds to save from ruin the formerly glorious Roland Garros Stadium and to increase the prize money so that the winners in singles stood to earn a million and a half francs. Having conquered the elusive stars with these idealistic inducements, Chatrier persuaded both the national television station and the foreign networks to cover the tournament in its entirety.

The feminists also owe him a laurel wreath: he was one of the first to propose equal prize money for women and men. But to acquire these goodies, the professionals have to arm themselves with saintly patience, for the clay courts at Roland Garros are the world's most grueling. It takes an expert tactician to avoid having one's tongue hang out by the end of the first set. My maestro Jimmy Connors, for example, never won the French title. Come to think of it, the Countess had been astute in equipping her warrior daughter with a private physician to do battle in this slaughter house.

Monsieur Chatrier had us dine in the tent with the Lacostes, whose sport-shirt logo, the green crocodile, must be crying real tears, thinking about the millions it has brought to the family. The table was graced by Jerry Lewis, who happened to be passing through Paris and who told some gloriously irreverent jokes about his colleague Ronald Reagan—jokes I won't repeat here to avoid the extra accusation of treason. The tent, right at courtside, may have been improvised, but not the chef: the oysters melted in your mouth, the *fois gras* was indescribably delicate, the triumphant salads were bathed in vinagrettes with untold fragrances, and the *sanglant* filets were so tender, a baby could have eaten them. About the wines I prefer not to go into detail. For the purposes of this tale it matters only that as the evening wore on a spark was ignited in my eyes and my lips, accelerating my German and English and leading me to commit an act of folly every three minutes. The last of these took place when Sophie's mother escorted her back to the hotel and I followed her, in the open air. It was not my fault that the sky was studded with stars, nor that Sophie reclined on the pedestal of an imitation Greek statue, nor that she closed her eyes, the better to hear the crickets rubbing their legs, nor that from the tent came wafting a gentle sax version of a Charles Trenet melody.

Her mother must have been exchanging addresses with her old friends or powdering her nose in the bathroom, and perhaps it was the moment to act upon my interpretation of Milosz's poem.

On the brink of hurling myself into the abyss, I was overcome by
the infantile terror of having misunderstood everything, of making
a fool of myself at fifty-two years of age, of being rejected with a
shocked grimace or—worse—a chuckle, and above all—it was the
strangest feeling—of seeing my cherished illusion brusquely ter-
minated.

*   *   *

Two hours after this incident, as I was hastening to set the
alarm in order to arrive punctually at Sophie's first match, sched-
uled for ten in the morning, who should appear in my room but the
Duchess von Mass? She was followed by a bellboy bearing a pail
of ice, two fluted glasses, and the unmistakable little head of Dom
Perignon peering out from under the folds of the napkin that
covered the pail. To be fair to Diana von Mass, if it was true that
one could be devoured, bones and all, by her acid tongue, it was no
less true that one could at times find oneself the beneficiary of her
magnanimity. She was many things but not stingy. She had put me
up at the Ritz, where my father-in-law would not have taken a room
without giving his bank account a coronary arrest. On a calling
card she informed me that starting tomorrow I had at my disposal
a chauffer-driven limousine, and on top of that very message—in
the manner of a paperweight—she had placed a flask of Iranian
caviar with a silver spoon, suggesting the childish prospect of
going at the little eggs straight from the jar, as if one were dealing
with blackberry jam. She was wearing the same skirt she wore at
the dinner, but she had changed her blouse and had renounced her
arsenal of jewels. Her slender, bare neck extended to the beginning
of her breasts, which a maliciously unfastened button could not
hide. She looked even younger than Ana, and, considering things
objectively, any courtier would be in his glory receiving in his
room at that hotel that woman with that champagne.

"I've come to thank you for everything you've done for
Sophie," she said while uncorking the champagne, not allowing
me to help her.

"No need for that."

"I spoke on the phone with your father-in-law and unfor-tunately have some bad news."

"I should know of it at once."

"He appreciates the gentility of your helping Sophie, but both he and his daughter are incensed about your lie. Why did you tell them you were coming here to some kind of institute for venereal diseases?"

"Tropical diseases."

"The things you come up with are tropical. Why are you lying like a traumatized child? What's wrong with your accepting a professional assignment in a foreign country for a few days? I hope it's clear that you can name your fee!"

"Thank you, Diana."

"Don't thank me for anything. Tell me why you lied."

She looked at me threateningly, and I peered over at her, trying to see through her expression whether she already knew the answer and only wanted to expose me to the same ridicule I had tried meticulously to avoid two hours before with her daughter. For these difficult cases, Harvard etiquette recommends looking concertedly at the tips of your shoes until your interlocutor reinitiates the conversation. I did so with painful consequences. The noose of guilt seemed to take shape, extending from a rafter of the roof as the seconds passed. But as the siege of Diana's glance did not diminish, it dawned on me that the real reason for her visit was Sophie, and fortunately (with the help of that infernal button) I came up with a diversionary military strategy to put me out of firing range.

"This champagne is an elixir of the gods," I said. "I'm afraid you are already spending the prize money Sophie has yet to earn."

"A million and a half francs," she said with a sigh.

I figured Countess von Mass would be sensitive to such matters.

"A tasty tidbit!"

"A *boccato dei cardinali*, Raymond!"

"I can imagine all those bills piled one on top of the other. They would form a tower more or less this high, don't you think?"

"Do you find me to be too materialistic?"

"I find you, rather, to be of exquisite material."

"Doctor Papst, do you, besides barking, bite at times?"

I thought it prudent to leave this query unanswered. If I said "I bite" I could only encourage her down two paths that were very dangerous for me: either to throw me the bone—something that did not suit me since my body and soul were not in that state—or to alert her as to the possibility of my assailing her daughter. In this second case I had no problem with my body and soul but plenty of problems with my morals, civil state, professional obligations, age, and horror at being wrong, among other shortcomings. On the other hand, stating "I don't bite" relegated me to the dustbin of the dull and the cynical. Ergo, I finished off the first glass of champagne and immediately served myself another. She imitated me and stretched out her arm, asking for a refill.

"Raymond," she said. "I've had a very hard life."

I made a remorseful face and tried to support that sentence by forgetting we were at the Ritz, enjoying Dom Perignon and Iranian caviar, and decked out in fashions by Cacharel and Christian Dior, respectively.

"Ever since Sophie was born I have had to be both father and mother for her, and I don't think I've succeeded in both tasks. It is true that we are on the eve of her greatest athletic feats, and I know I've played a decisive role in her professional formation. But, on the other hand, I've uprooted Sophie from everything that makes a teenager's life normal: she has no home, no friends, no father, and finally I had to decide two years ago to take her out of school. Her education has been practically nil."

"Nonetheless, she seems very sensitive to me. I'm under the impression that she likes poetry."

Not even during the dinner with Jerry Lewis did I hear such thunderous laughter.

"Poetry, Raymond Papst! Sophie hasn't picked up a book in her whole life. When she reads sports magazines she has to sound out one syllable at a time by pointing with her finger. She's as refined as a cement slab."

She drained the second glass with a gulp and began to play

with her unfastened button. "But she is beautiful," she concluded funereally.

"Beautiful," I agreed.

"I have to chase away her admirers as if I were sweeping cockroaches. I don't like to do it, but tennis requires a temper of steel. It has become a sport of children, and I know full well that both our economic futures depend on whatever she may achieve between now and when she is twenty-three. That fainting spell in Berlin, Doctor, had something to do with a man."

Despite the champagne and the Lacostes' wine, I felt my head clear. Nothing more instructive than one's own interests.

"How so?" I asked, surprised, scandalized.

"She's smitten by this Spanish playboy."

"Is she in love with him?"

"Sophie is too young to love, don't you think?"

"I don't see what one thing has to do with the other."

"This young man has made some awful scenes in hopes of getting her into bed."

"My God!"

"He takes her to discotheques where they drink champagne and smoke that filth. That night in Berlin, for the first time I lost track of my daughter. I didn't know where she was until she appeared on the court."

I filled our glasses with more champagne. Diana interpreted this gesture as paternal solidarity and anxiously squeezed my forearm.

"You think," I said, "that that night was (any phrase seemed either vulgar or corny to me, and I opted for the corny) 'a night of love.'"

"No, go on! Sophie is a complete virgin."

This time it was she who filled my glass.

"I was on the verge of losing her when you, Doctor Papst, happened into our lives. She loves you and respects you, and between affection and love ..."

"What do you mean?" I murmured, between fearful and flattered.

"Let's dispense with the rhetoric, Doctor Papst. Sophie

and I need you at this moment in our lives. Having never had a father, it is not strange that she develop toward you a sort of affection that you could manipulate."

"I don't see what in my behavior could induce you to so aggressive a judgment."

"Nothing, but it would be catastrophic for Sophie to be tying the dog up with sausages."

"Countess, you have specialized in canine imagery."

"Don't distract me from what I want to tell you. Approach her like a doctor, but leave her like a man. If you don't proceed as I suggest to you, you will find yourself confronted by more than just my tongue."

"I am so charmed in the vertigo of your obscenities, Madame, that I permit myself to ask what you insinuate by that remark."

I thought it wise to put an end to this intimidation with non-verbal methods. I went over to the door to the hall and opened it wide in an inviting gesture. Diana made a mental calculation of the alternatives, raised the bottle of Dom Perignon to see how much was left, served the rest into the two glasses, and came over with them to me. We drank in silence without looking each other in the eye. After a while she took the famous button between two finger nails, opening and closing it as if keeping rhythm with her heart-beat.

"Doctor Papst, I want to tell you that I like you a lot."

"Any objective bystander would say that it doesn't show."

*   *   *

As the tournament drew toward its conclusion, my fragile fortune was threatened not only by my fears but also by the frontal offensive mounted by my father-in-law and Ana, both informed in detail by the German press, which outdid itself in praising its starlet, for whom I was head physician.

This *head*, of course, was written in italics so everyone would understand head of the bed. Ten percent of the comments written about the princess's glorious ascent were dedicated to me with the ambiguous sympathy reserved for one who has helped a compatriot, but who at the same time occupies a privileged place at her side: an illegitimate usurpation of the dreams of tens of thousands of Germans who like to think of their idols as members of the family. I imagine that explains the enthusiasm with which they espouse the most extravagant ideas. Be that as it may, these texts were child's play, adventures with little paper airplanes, compared to the turbulence of the suicide flights in the offing.

My father-in-law fired telegrams, cables, Telex and Fax messages, and close friends among the French nobility at me. The messages varied, but the contents were constant: *come back, you son of a bitch.* Ana, imperturbably proud, had sent only one normal letter, of a half page in length, which took three days to reach me. She thanked me for the Pakistanis' marvelous health certificate, informed me about a photographic reproduction of a giant tapestry by Jackson Pollock that seemed real in the avant-garde gallery's catalogue, expressed some slight satisfaction over the lyrical excesses of Abbado's direction of the Brahms at the Philharmonic, referred cordially to the gesture of "your colleague Mollenhauer's accompanying me to the concert, trying clumsily to compensate for your painful absence," and concluded by begging me to notify her of the day and time of my return flight so she could prepare me a home-cooked meal. Not even the faintest reference to Sophie Mass or her mother, despite the growing space our pictures occupied in the German newspapers and weekly magazines as Sophie advanced steadily toward the finals.

The day she qualified for the finals by defeating an American opponent in three heart-rending sets, a formal dance was organized to benefit the reconstruction of the Roland Garros, an event that gave me the opportunity to dust off my tux.

An orchestra that imitated perfectly the Latin American combos of the forties played the Roberto Lecaros tune "You Must Know I Love You and Don't Love You," and I got lost in the intimate sound of the muted trumpet that resembled a human voice in its relaxed phrasing. Phrasing. I adore this favorite term jazz musicians use to describe the indefinable mixture of personality, originality, distortion, and emotive tone with which a singer or instrumentalist interprets a theme. I isolate a word since once again I want to isolate a person: Sophie Mass. Sophie phrased her beauty with the same naturalness with which a swimmer breathes. There was a style and spontaneity about her, a grace few achieve. An excess of emphasis on style leads to artifice, too much accent on the spontaneous comes down to coarseness. That gala night there were two stars of the first magnitude: the ones who had made it to the finals, to be disputed the next afternoon. One was of course our Sophie, and the other was a seasoned maestra of Czech origin who resides in the United States. The rest of the competitors had departed for lesser tournaments, but the tables were filled with noteworthy parties from diverse spheres. The celebration took place in the Ritz itself, in a salon decorated with mirrors and furniture brought from the Windsor Haus. Countess von Mass's tactics were worthy of inclusion in the annals of great public relations firms. It is true she had a backlog of ire accumulated against the aristocracy, but she knew how to administer it in a captivating and provocative way. She made each group of aristo-crats feel she was happy with the noble attitude they had struck in not adding to the gossip and calumnies. A few days later I discovered the favorite phrase she dealt them all was: "Dearie, how grateful I am for the moral support you have given me all these terrible years." With a variant: "Dearie, Sophie's triumph is in part your own triumph." I was witness to this line dropped in the prominent left earlobe of Mohammed al-Fayad, the Ritz's multi-millionaire Egyptian owner, who sponsored us to a table illumi-nated with such mathematical precision that it went with Sophie's jewels and dress. Impossible to say who would win Sunday's finals, but the psychological drubbing tendered to the Czech player through the Countess von Mass's *mise-en-scène* must have made her feel like a failed Cinderella, whose rags would not be trans-formed into an evening dress, and for whom no prince charming or sulky with spirited steeds would come to take her to the hotel bridal suite. After the dinner, Sophie circulated among all the tables receiving praise and congratulations. Just when they finished "You Must Know I Love You and Don't Love You" she began her walk toward us, pursued by a handsome young man with the look of a race-car driver. To see her approach (I felt like saying "to see her materialize") was the same as hearing the crescendo of a Romantic symphony.

Throwing all caution to the wind, I turned in a state toward her mother:

"Sophie is a miracle!"

The Countess raised one eyebrow and dealt me a wry smile as direct as a fist to the jaw.

"It's a miracle I can explain to you rationally: dress by Christian Lacroix, handbag by Judith Leiber, necklace by Cartier, Lancomes's Rouge à Lèvres Satin in Le Red, and makeup by Olivier Echaudemaison. German shoes."

"And how much does the investment come to?"

"Forty-five thousand francs."

*   *   *

Sophie sauntered the last few meters looking straight into my eyes, her smile widening as she drew nearer. I had the impression that her loquacious interlocutor was speaking in the void. Then the most flattering thing happened. She extended her bare hand to me and said:

"Is it unseemly for a patient to ask her doctor to dance?"

I couldn't leave that renowned hand floating in the air. I took it gently and, after smiling at her mother and anonymous suitor, I answered:

"No, but my worries have me paralyzed. And the salon is full of less moldy rackets than I. Like this young beau."

I gestured toward the fortunate courtier with the strong chin, but Sophie paid him no attention. Awash in spontaneity and imprudence, she said peremptorily, in front of her mother:

"Are you afraid to hold me?"

Since the answer was yes, I said:

"No."

"So?"

"My dear, I am here to take care of you, not to shake you up."

But Sophie pulled me up by the hand and led me to the dance floor, where the back of my neck received the darting stares of all those in attendance, but especially of one, whose barbs seemed patented: the Countess's. When you're at sea, however, there's nothing to do but swim. Sophie had the good sense not to do anything provocative during the first minute. But as soon as other couples joined in and the spotlight was deflected slightly from us, she rested her head on my chest and, rubbing her lips on the lapel of my dinner jacket, she began to blow on it, producing that heat children call fire.

"I'm a dragon," she said.

A redeeming sentence to distance me from the obsessive concentration with which my body felt every particle of hers as we danced. "A fire-breathing dragon." How I allowed myself to be fooled by the princess's mundane and manorial appearance! She was nothing but a child! The excitement of her triumph did not give her more gravity; it gave her wings, and she expressed her glee through games proper to a Christmas party. Nonetheless, the breathing gambit was her idea, and air is a god who brings news of our most unfathomable depths. Almost confirming my line of thought, she rose high on her "German shoes" and put her lips next to my ear to confide:

"I want to tell you something."

"What?" I said, looking in the direction of her mother's table.

"This."

And she blew a slight gust of air over my earlobe, and then aimed her breath behind my pinna, and afterwards brought it to the upper folds, only to puff with her lips almost to my eardrum.

"Sophie," I said.

Without leaving my ear, almost as if she were nibbling on it with her deafeningly mischievous teeth, she murmured:

"Raymond, you're as stiff as a board."

"Frankly, dancing was never my forte."

"I wasn't referring to that."

"Let's go back to the table."

"Only a boor would leave me alone in the middle of the

dance floor before the music finished."

"Enough of your games, then."

"I never play games, Raymond."

"And what is it you're doing?"

"Waiting."

No, my angel; I was not going to ask for what. That word could shoot me down a slide to my ruin. Even if the answer were moderately favorable to me, I was a prisoner of my status and my inhibitions.

"To relieve your tensions?"

"Me, tense?"

"Wouldn't you like to escape from this mausoleum and find some place with live music?"

"What you call live music kills me."

She lay her mother-of-pearl handbag on my tuxedo jacket and, frowning like a spoiled little girl, she sighed:

"I'm fed up with living like this."

"Like what?"

"My mother treats me as if I were made of glass that someone or something could break at any moment. I hardly enjoy playing tennis any more. Everything is discipline, training, hotels, courts, airplanes."

"Admirers."

"There's no time to get to know anyone. If you like someone, when he calls you for a date you're already at the airport or in some other city. Tennis players sleep only with their rackets."

To the list of credits for the title of Supreme Imbecile of the Republic, which sooner rather than later I will be awarded, I should add this adolescent phrase, uttered not by her but by me:

"And you?"

"Raymond Papst," she said amidst a laugh that dispersed all the intimacy built up till then. "What an impertinent question!"

"Foolish perhaps, but what's impertinent about two syllables?"

"Your question encourages me to ask you another one."

"Go ahead."

"What did my mother say to you?"

"She threatened me."

"And you?"

"Me?"

"What are planning to do?"

The music had stopped, and you could clearly hear the sound of the teaspoons stirring the cups of coffee, mixed with the jingle of the bracelets dangling from the exquisite and wealthy wrists. Sometimes you have to engage in silly prattle to come up with a second's inspiration.

"To wait," I said triumphantly, and now I certainly did undergird that term with an intention that was virile, solemn, expectant, superior.

It was a highly suspect moment. Embracing in the middle of the hall, without the orchestra to grace our silence, was an offense against discretion and prudence. But I couldn't let her go without a reply, even if it caused a scandal among the hundreds of people who were surely staring at us. When Sophie realized it was incumbent upon her to answer, and I in my nervousness was beginning to savor my victory, she came forward very slowly, deliberately, intensely, gently, her lips partly open as if set to kiss me on the mouth. I had no doubts as to the perturbing meaning of her gesture, and I was disposed to let her advance only a centimeter more before moving my face away in order to avoid the public embarrassment, when she halted her motion and said to me with an expression that aged her ten years:

"You're going to rot waiting, Raymond Papst."

*   *   *

Back in my room I divested myself of my dinner jacket as if I were extricating myself from the meticulous tentacles of an octopus. I was sweating, furious, sad, disconsolate. On top of the nightstand's rococo doily sat four or five telegrams, and under them a letter to which I paid no immediate attention. Some of the urgent messages came from Baron von Bamberg. Their contents were no different from those already mentioned, so I spare myself repeating the unpleasantries. One of them, however, proposed a variant: "Return Berlin discuss inheritance problem." I needed no course in hermeneutics in order to understand the implicit message: "Either you come home right now or I cut you off." Another little note signed by my colleague Mollenhauer, a virtuoso in knavishness: "Chaos, Mollenhauer."

When I was about to read the letter I noticed an intense focus of light panning across the curtains of my window. Curious, I turned off the table lamp and, pressing myself against the wall, I tried to spy outward while remaining unseen. It was a beam coming from a flashlight so powerful that I could not see who was handling it. To be sure, it occurred to me that it could be Sophie spreading in my direction another of her ambiguously playful nets, but I had had so many mistaken perceptions that I opted to disregard that idea. Nonetheless, I struck upon a plan to ascertain if the light was coming from her room. I slid toward the telephone and dialed her room number. With the first ring, the light changed direction and pointed toward the room's interior. When she lifted the receiver, I simply hung up. No more than a minute had passed and already the flashlight was again assailing my window with despairing intermittency, just what one would expect from a spoiled child who ceaselessly kicked the wall to annoy her parents.

I ostentatiously drew the delicate curtain, but that did not end the game. Even with that filter, the flashlight kept projecting spasmodically onto the baroque tapestry of the wall, like the replica of an excited heartbeat. Stretched across my bed I moved my head trying to imagine the lyrics to go with that syncope. It could be: "I love you, I love you, I love you." Or: "I hate you, I hate you, I hate you." Or: "Come, come, come." I closed my eyes. The flashes were still tenuously present on my retinas. I undid the buttons of my shirt and then those of my pants. For a while I distractedly twirled the hairs of my chest with my fingertips and then, fluidly, the same hand descended, rubbing across my skin, until alighting on my penis. I touched it almost with pity, with a sort of camaraderie that I had not shared with it since the fevers of my adolescence. Around the tender flesh the dampness had increased. Then I moved my arm toward the headboard and turned on the bedside lamp in order to ventilate my thoughts and banish my phantoms. That was the instant when I again saw the envelope.

The colored border around its edge was unusual for my correspondence: alternating red and yellow broken lines. Over a voluminous stamp with the effigy of Goya they had cancelled Cibeles and Madrid. On the right side a red sticker: *expreso*. Informal, though intelligible, calligraphy, and a meticulous exposition of the address of the Ritz, including its postal code and Telex number. I ripped open the envelope by making short, tearing motions with my fingernails, and upon unfolding the letter's three pages I searched avidly for the sender's signature. There in melancholy and rabid black was the name of Pablo Braganza. Above the surname the word *Yours* and below an address—in a nervous script—but also with the number of the mailing district.

I transcribe below the text just as I read it, omitting the emotions and judgments it provoked in me line by line and paragraph by paragraph.

Dr. Papst:

I have before me snapshots from Spanish and French newspapers in which you are shown pestering Sophie Mass. I imagine your recent behavior with the Countess has ensured you a place at the Court, and now I understand the enthusiasm, worthy of a small-time henchman, with which you undertook the ignoble task of separating me from my beloved. If I bared my passionate young heart before a physician like yourself, it was because I was hoping for guidance, understanding, solidarity, and especially help. You listened with Sephardic cunning to my afflictions, you learned of intimate matters that put me at risk, and although you used against me the word *bribery*, in the light of recent events it is clear that it was *you* who bribed me in order to tear me away from Sophie and pave the way toward her seduction. I see your image in the papers and, laying aside the repugnance your receding hairline causes me, take the liberty to draw your attention to the absurdity of your public figure.

If you prefer you may throw this paper into the waste basket or tear it into little pieces or grind it into particles. As a gesture of fair play, I warn you of its contents from the start: a description of

the events that night at the Kempinski after you took your leave
from the discotheque, and hours before Sophie fainted on the court
for reasons which you have probably explained to my beloved and
her mother with the gibberish of a tribal witch doctor. Now you
will know the truth contained in none of your books.

   We each drank our fill of champagne. I with the excess of
one smitten with both love and poetic frenzy (*sic: I fulfill my
promise not to intervene in the text*), she in the discrete doses
suggested by reason and training. At the club, people were dancing
according to the latest styles, but the subject of my chat was
Spanish Romantic poetry, especially the verses of Bécquer, and a
contemporary art show I had seen at the Reina Sofía Center in
Madrid and to which I planned to invite her before, *instead of*, or
after Paris.   I wanted her to see for herself those hallucinatory
pictures in which I had seen my love for her grow. Each of those
strokes of vibrant oil expressed a nuance of my passion. During my
long days in those salons, I discovered that a man in amatory
suspension rescues or demands love from all things.   Sophie
possesses something that characterizes the ineffable work of art,
and in that gallery I wanted to show her with images the truth of her
soul; a sun would dawn in my beloved's mind, she would shed the
bonds of her provincial mooring, her eyes would fill with stars and
every mysterious pleat of her soul would overflow with freedom;
she would cease to be the tame and consumable idol for millions
who long only to measure her with their diminished staffs, use her
up with their cheap genuflections, exploit her for their Sunday
leisure, their mediocre press, their tin cups, sneakers and copy-
righted rackets.

   I imagined that she strolled those galleries with me and that
in the secluded silence, filtered this time through her eyes, I would
find the image that would allow me to anoint, febrile and devout,
an exorcizing word upon her lips. Sophie is a woman and a
mystery.   An enormous enigma like a country with crowded
avenues, side streets, surreptitious paths, hidden barrens, abysses
and mountain ranges (sic).   She *is and is not* aware of that
mysterious radiance. Her athletic talent blocks her access to that
domain where the sleeping angel awaits the kiss of the prince who

will save her from the curse. She knows she is wonderful. But she thinks it is her status as a tennis star that explains and exhausts her magic. That is why I have struggled with a lover's tenacity to indicate to her the path of freedom. And there is no other way to be free than to immerse oneself in the marvelous vertigo of art and poetry where a good metaphor and a shining word mean more than life and bread. I have regaled her with books about art, cassettes and records of my favorite compositions, an original sketch by Picasso, and especially poetry, none of those improvised or pretentious verses written by pretentious youths who wish to forget, but those that connect man with his past, his myths, his gods, that poetry where eternity vibrates and transports you in an epic rhythm, in a meditation that wraps our insignificant present in a halo of transcendence. Among other authors, we have read together Saint John Perse, Seferis, Milosz, Hölderlin, and Emily Dickinson, names which, to be sure, will mean nothing to someone like you, mired in your struggle for money and for a vicarious notoriety wheedled in the shadow of Sophie's success. You finally have what you were looking for, Doctor Papst. These pictures in the papers assure you the crumb of publicity you sought.

Now you can discreetly retire to your office, label the pictures where chance put you at her side, and brag to your inhibited patients about the adventure you never had.

That night we spoke of Gustavo Adolfo Bécquer, of his delicacy, of the lightness with which he expresses in rhymed and harmonious letter everything that in him is blood and turbulence. I could not render in German what in Castilian was the breath of a soul. I also gave her a book of verses by my favorite poet: Milosz.

Sophie then danced a couple of numbers with some delinquent while I was lacerated by the horror of having another man touch her. I was held in the grips of a boundless depression. You laughed at my mind-altering pills and my revolver and made me feel like a clown or some hysterical teenager. If you only knew, though, with what intimate conviction I acquired both tools. How could I prove to Sophie that if every minute away from her was a knife cutting into my veins and bleeding me dry, the fact that another made physical contact with her skin was something so burning that it resembled an agony? (sic) I had to tell it to her *radically* in the only language a *radical* love can understand: death. Upon returning to the table I refused to look at her, but she, angelic, intuitive, with that sharpness for capturing the crucial moments and distinguishing the frivolous from the essential, said to me, taking my hand, *let's go to your hotel.*

As soon as we entered, she leaned against the wall, curving her belly slightly outward. I unburdened myself of my jacket, throwing it on the rug, and standing in front of her, I drew my mouth near to kiss her. Sophie interposed her extended hand, and my lips had to console themselves with brushing against her knuckles. When I removed her fingers, I looked at her fixedly, searching for a way to please her. She had dropped her arms as a sign of surrender, her neck tilted tenderly over one shoulder. I wanted to open her blouse without hiding the excitement of an anticipated image: my delicately biting one of her nipples. But Sophie detained my action, this time with no physical obstacles: she limited herself to nodding no with her head. Again the same anxiety, again the disconcertion. It was then that she imposed her conditions. She did it with a gesture not in the slightest ambiguous, but one which at first I resisted taking literally.

She had lowered her gaze slowly toward my pants and held it at my crotch. My impassivity, purely the product of my disconcertion, did not seem to vex her, but after half a minute one of her hands rose to my hair, insinuated itself in that luxuriance, and with an unmistakable gesture pressed down on my head, indicating that I should kneel. Once lowered and trembling with delight (sic), I sunk my hands under her skirt and without touching her thighs I seized with my fingernails the elastic of her brief panties and pulled them down to her knees while she helped their displacement by moving her thighs together. When the garment dangled between her knees, I placed my index finger on top and slid it down to the high heels of her shoes. She culminated the process by removing the shoe from one foot, lifting her panties with her middle finger, and throwing them to one side. The light silk skirt hid that new nudity and I could not resist the madness of kissing her belly through it. I advanced my lips over the skirt and through them felt the first emotion of the thickness of her pubic hair. It was she who raised the skirt right away, offering at a minimum distance the unforeseen spectacle of her sex. Balancing myself over the fragile thread of a spider web, I stretched the tenuously pink skin around her clitoris, over which, after focusing on its volume, I moved my tongue, moistening it with my thick saliva and then squeezing it against my lips, as I inhaled the aroma emanating from that whole area.

Afterwards I licked it for her (sic) with a serenity that belied my violent heart, without her changing her position against the wall, without her rotating her hips, without her emitting a sound other than that of breathing, which seemed to detect every nuance of my touch on her flesh. She did not caress my hair, nor did her hands come to coordinate the lack or excess of pressure from my tongue. One could say that at that moment she dispensed with my body and her own. In the absolute of that moment the only things that existed were her clitoris and my tongue. If I was under that sweet yoke five minutes or ten, I cannot tell. I yearned to take her, to pour her onto the bed and anoint her with my saliva and my agitated semen from her fibula to her eyelashes, but I did not dare break the spell, and her peacefulness and conformity were imperious. After a long time, there was a sort of spasm in her abdomen and then her hands certainly did press down upon my head and her voice, suddenly hoarse, said:

"Now!"

And she added:

"Find me, find me!"

Inspiration led me to join my lips with my tongue and, rubbing with both, my eyes blurred with tears, I intensified the speed and pressure, until she shouted *my love*, shook in submission to the undulations of her orgasm, and with the palm of her hand on my forehead separated me like a slave asking for a truce.

Should I provide you with more details of this day, Doctor Papst?

Do you want to know how many more words of love her mouth poured out that night? Need I specify in what physical circumstances these were pronounced?

I will show the gentility of sparing you them. But I cannot help but tell you that from that night of poetry and sex there was born between the two of us an intimate bond that will make all other relationships pale as insufficient, ridiculous, and anecdotal; you will never win her love!

You contrived to separate me from her, you jumped on her mother's wagon, with her petulant ambitions of fame and her artificial friendships, her foolishness of kinglets and buffoons, her accumulation of rings that like parasites strangle her fingers, her necklaces that fail to hide the horrible crevices of her wrinkles. Maybe Sophie will win the French Open! But what will she do then? Do you think she will continue to spend her life looking across a net? With me she knew emotions that your years, Doctor Papst, will not give her; electric volts of poetry and passion that your routinized imagination cannot conceive. I know the attraction I hold for her. Here, as always, love will triumph. Allow me to close with some of Quevedo's verses:

> *"So much land and so many seas*
> may come between us,
> may my fire set aside,
> *but will not temper my fire."*

Yours,

Pablo Braganza

*   *   *

I stumbled toward the bathroom overtaken by a sudden blindness, a disturbance that did not allow me to coordinate my movements. My temples tense, an unfamiliar sweat on my brow. Decency bids me to pass over my other physical manifestations at this point. I put my head under the cold water tap and ran the water over my neck and hair for a long time.

Delirious, I rubbed my eyelids.

I spat violently against the wall, assailed by the images of his letter. Of his *report*, I corrected. I could not think about this compulsion. I dried the perspiration on my chest with the curtain that faced the interior patio. The flashing lights had ceased. Sophie's room was dark. Could she be inside, still possessed by the same whims that gnawed at her slumber? Could she have fallen asleep like a healthy baby, her retinas filled with scenes in which she was triumphant in Sunday's finals? Or could she have thrown her body adrift onto the discotheque dance floor, waiting for any passing sailor to blow his Pernaud breath on her earlobes?

In order to save myself, I had to write. Tomorrow, in a week, in a year I would perhaps see the letter's psychopathic pettiness, but now I had to return that *brulote*, that exhibitionistic gambit, by means of a poetic blow that would execute the beardless lad with his own weapons. I weigh this metaphorical sentence on the scale of present reality and regret its inopportune and prophetic quality, but I submit it with the usual rigor, which I hope to turn into a method. I do not write to please myself or to compensate for what reality has not allowed me to be, but I do it to undeceive myself, to lash my illusions, to smash the masks. I do not want to fall into that vice of conceiving of oneself as different or distinct from what one really is.

I took hold of my fountain pen, with which I had etched a comfortable life by filling out stupid prescriptions, and I wrote the following reply on stationery bearing the Ritz letterhead:

Señor
Pablo Braganza:

I read your boasts distractedly. Since you are interested in poetry and are already a bit familiar with its more histrionic facets, I take the liberty of sending you this sentence from a letter Rilke, while residing in Spain, wrote to Rodin, in the hope that you grasp my indifference to your braggadocio:

"One might say that an objectless, but never inactive, heroism has formed Spain: she arises, she grows tense, she exaggerates, she provokes heaven, and heaven, from time to time, to please her, rises in anger and answers with gestures of clouds, but

this amounts to no more than a generous and useless spectacle."
I also close in the manner of Rilke: with a firm handshake,
Yours,

Raymond Papst

I called the switchboard and asked for a bellboy to pick up
the note. I told him to send it special delivery and, if he did not mind
making a second trip to my room, to return bringing a bottle of *Ritz
Piccolo* champagne. Having completed this transaction, and
consequently having decided upon the contents of the bottle, I clad
myself in my Italian shoes, my father-in-law's tuxedo, and my
Harvard bow tie, and with Ana's wedding ring on my finger, I
headed, with all the sanity of a lunatic, toward the elevator that
would take me to Sophie's room. I had not smoked for years, but
I would have given my father-in-law's gold-plated walking stick
for a cigarette. At full speed, as if rhythm nullified prudence, I
proceeded vigorously toward her door, and I knocked with the
typical discretion of one who has clandestine intentions. For one
minute I waited for the door to open, and upon seeing there was no
response, I returned to my room, doffed the Italian shoes, stripped
off the father-in-law's tux, peeled off the Harvard bow tie, and
unfettered myself of Ana's ring, and sinking between the sheets I
touched my phallus.

*   *   *

The breakfasts served at the Ritz are gargantuan. Every
guest every morning of every month of every year—says the
brochure—ought to feel what it's like to emerge from a wedding
night. Eggs in silver goblets, fruits cosmetically touched up to
luminescent perfection, the irresistible texture of the *bas-reliefs* on
the tea sets, subtly embroidered napkin hems, and the bottle of
Piccolo, Diana von Mass's gesture of gentility. That was the
golden frame in which I reread Pablo Braganza's summation of
allegations, this time without inflamed emotions, trying to distinguish the sound from the fury, in order to detect how many stones

the river had really churned up.

I brushed aside the first accusations against me—blackmail and social climbing—since one did not concern me and the other, while partially true, did not play a major role in this case. That I was depraved was given the lie by the transparent fact that I had not so much as kissed Sophie, or any female of that age for thirty-two years. My thoughts, those phantasms with their lubricious gestures, were, of course, another matter.

Young Braganza's caricaturesque portrayals of my lewdness were a free transposition of scenes from Goya. They simply did not fit me, even in my wildest moments of self-destruction.

The charming little letter began to interest me only after the introduction, from the moment when it presented two great themes: 1.) what Papst has gotten from Sophie Mass, and 2.) the night of love at the Kempinski that unleashed this story, this trip, and, why not say it, this *dementia*.

I immersed myself in the complexities of number *one*, caressing a California orange as plump as a watermelon, a detail that seemed to suggest a joke about the Ritz's opulence, and within a minute I reached the following conclusion: Braganza was on the mark. Except for problems, Doctor Papst had neither asked for nor obtained ANYTHING from Sophie Mass. Point, game, and set for my young rival.

Theme *two* was immensely more intricate and diffuse. Cartesian logic recommended a prudent dissection into subthemes in order to reach clear and distinct conclusions. Let's consider, then, *2a.* and dedicate ourselves to the subcomplex of poetry. I laugh myself silly at the ridiculous prospect of uncovering someone's intimate being by applying an anthology of contemporary poetry, as one might give electroshocks to a schizophrenic. Rather than accost his beloved with verses, the lad ought to have learned something of the rhetoric of the poets he cites, so as not to incur such sappy phrases as *A sun would dawn in my beloved's mind, she would shed the bonds of her provincial mooring, her eyes would fill with stars*. I know very well—since learning it from the widow González—that when a man is aroused even his bladder waxes poetic, but surely it was the metaphorical diarrhea with which he assailed Sophie that had caused her fainting on the court, rather than young Dr. Higgins's sexual performance.

Of theme two, then, what was painfully salvageable was to learn that Milosz's marvelous poem, with which little Sophie had unsettled me, originated in the poetic dilettantism of her young suitor. I could not avoid feeling rage at lurid images in which the poem, carried about in sleeplessness, appeared spotted with drops of my opponent's sperm. So her mother was right. Sophie did not understand the first thing about poetry. Granted: but how she administered that ignorance!

Let us now deal with the issue of the night of love.

First question: Why did he tell me about it?

Answer: To prove Sophie belonged to him. That he pretended to have dominated her poetically was clear. Regarding physical possession, the missive gave to understand that he drove her crazy, debilitating her with pleasure, and that his instrument (endowed with untold virtues) was the magic wand that had captivated her. Modesty and objectivity aside, as my grandmother used to say.

The wand would then be the reason for her fainting on the court, and not the arguments that I had wielded "with the gibberish of a tribal witch doctor." It seems the youth placed more faith in the seductive virtues of this instrument than in his library, for he had emphasized the former rather than the latter in his famous farewell at the Berlin airport. Besides showing bad taste, that scuffle gave less than exhaustive information about the attributes of which he seemed to brag.

Ergo, one would have to search through the extensive letter for the wand's prowess during that night of love. Surprise: although the description of the erotic scenes tends toward minute precision, the personage who ought to occupy the leading role—the baby at the baptism, the corpse at the funeral—is not mentioned even once, nor is it insinuated that it entered into action. Rather, the hero of the battle was a tongue, a supple *heroine*, which I have nothing against, but in that department the nightingales tend to grow more and more sage with time.

If he denigrated my age by contrasting it with his fleeting

adolescence, just as in poker, he had to show something more than a simple pair of jokers. I reinforced these thoughts with a swallow of champagne and the memory of a delicious translation into English of an erotic Mexican poem in which the interpreter had had the good fortune to confuse the Spanish word *lengua, tongue*, with the English word *language*. The results were striking: *language* was capable of erotic feats that young Pablo, addicted to these in both senses, would have found to embody the ideal synthesis of poetry and sex.

Besides, the stage of this night of love was, to say the least, peculiar. In a place of the Kempinski's calibre, to limit oneself to a few square centimeters of wall (there being in the hotel and the city more than enough walls to go around) was shortsighted. I do not deny that toward the letter's end Pablo suggests he omits other incidents in order considerately to spare me pain, but he remembers to be lavish in his report when the woman of my sleepless nights has—or feigns having—a Hollywood-style orgasm.

I admit a bit of vitriol in my first conclusion: if the loquacious and lyrophonous Pablo Braganza tells no more it is because of that night there is *nothing more* to tell.

Even though the final match would begin in an hour, I took another glance at the text, proposing another hypothesis. The young man not only does not tell the truth when he says he is omitting things, he also omits the truth when he claims to be telling the story. In plain English: except for a minor fuss over the vial of deadly aspirins, and a click or two of an unloaded revolver, that night saw no other orgasm or climax.

What was, then, his goal in proferring me not a document—which, to be sure, had accomplished the night before the mission of irritating me down to the colon—but a piece of fiction whose shortcomings were his own and whose merits were not?

Answer replete with triumphant kettledrums, trumpets, and clarions: the young lover knew through Sophie that it was me, the very same Doctor Papst, whom she loved, and he presumed that, with my being in Paris with the woman of his dreams, what he wrote *to have happened* with him *would happen* with me. In this sense, his text was a sort of incense-burning smokescreen, something like a spell, a curse, a talisman that would keep me from having what he desired and could not have. If so, his behavior was pretty irrational, since a text like his might function as an antidote, but it could also act as a stimulus.

There was something unreal in the love scene's choreography. On further consideration, the extravagance of Sophie's opting for the upright position, along with her tenacity in not allowing herself to be kissed on the lips and proffering instead her sex, had a fantastic and even poetic quality. In denying the physical appropriation of something so exposed as her mouth, she made private and unreachable something normally public. Not a bad strategy for an idol. Pablo's letter never spoke of kissing her. Since the young man compared Sophie with natural images worthy of *National Geographic*, it is fitting to say she may have accorded him a superficial excursion along a "secret path," but clearly he had not scaled the mountain peak, much less plumbed the vertigo of her abyss.

Summarizing. If the young man's report did not lie, Sophie had put on a charade, establishing herself as enigmatic, sovereign despite her age, and violently erotic. If the described scene was, on the contrary, a literary invention of Braganza's, one had to admit that, by pruning its grosser metaphors, one could eventually reach an idea of some poetic value.

I went about peeling the orange, which in truth I had no intention of eating, to work off some of the energy accumulated in speculating on the missive's truth. This was my final reflection before heading for the court.

The longest paragraph consisted of an account of states of mind, situations, and an action. Everything was mediated by the author, who accented one thing or another, painted with his metaphors certain moments in the belief that he made them thus sublime, and again and again, with that self-centeredness I had detected in Berlin, called attention to the quality of his performance. OK, then, there was only one moment in which one had direct access to the voice of his novel's feminine character, and this was just at the threshold of her supposed orgasm. Her words then are *my love* and, curiously, *find me, find me.* Although it is an abominable exercise in the obvious, Pablo has this text stand out unmediated since he wants to let me know that *he* was the one who was designated by Sophie's elusive mouth as *my love* and to suggest at the same time that the beautiful *find me, find me* culminated when his labial artistry, moved by "inspiration," had indeed *found* her.

Consistent with my dialectic, I proposed not to question the veracity of his testimony but to interpret the facts just as they were represented, but in a different way. I am embarrassed to attack with pedestrian logic Sophie's or Braganza's poetic expression of that eagerness for pleasure in the metaphysical words *find me, find me*, but just as a kind of exercise I interpreted the four words emitted by her (four, since the verb in its imperative form and the direct object are repeated, changing, to be sure, the effective value of the utterance) in the following manner:

Sophie finds herself in a fix in the room at the Kempinski. Things turn violent.

A tug-o'-war with clothes ensues, with threats and weakness on both sides.

Brute force imposes itself, the girl feels defenseless.

In anguish she cries out for help.

She calls for her love—not the man who now accosts her— to protect and defend her.

Find me, find me—following the logic of this line of thought—is not said to someone who is there, present in the flesh, but to a distant person whose company is urgently desired.

The alternative interpretation goes this far. I admit that, *prima facie*, there is something farfetched, if not arbitrary, about it. I would share this criticism if it were not for the context we know of: the next day Sophie faints and *asks me* to intervene in order to free her from the young blackmailer. She asks *me* to do it. That is, the person who had appeared at the horrible discotheque to protect her, the same man who had shown his enrapturement on the tennis court, that being to whom on the dance floor she had already opened her arms in a gesture anticipatory of that *find me, find me*. If love and sex had been as satisfying and joyful as Pablo had painted them, why the deuce was she begging me only hours after that nightmarish evening to remove that obstacle from her path?

Poor Sophie! And right now, alone on the tennis court only moments before the final match, did she not need me, while I, like a man obsessed, read fantasies about her instead of enjoying her *real* presence in Paris? As something of a good omen I found among the sweets a portion of *Bienenstich*. In keeping with a deeply ingrained tradition, I ate it on the way.

*   *   *

The match had begun with frightful punctuality, and when I saw the scoreboard I could scarcely believe my eyes. Sophie was already losing, two games to love. If for an amateur it is serious to have your service broken in the opening minutes, for a professional it is fatal, especially in the final round of a Grand Slam tournament. Her rival was an American who paced up and down the base line like a lioness, instilling terror with her mere presence. She was not chewing gum, but she may as well have been. When I sat down on the bench next to the Countess, Sophie spotted me. She grew so still while looking in my direction that her opponent, who was about to serve, halted her action, put her hands on her waist, and turned her gaze to where Sophie was staring. Within ten seconds I had the entire stadium's eyes upon me. In my discomfort I adjusted an imaginary tie about my neck.

I snapped my fingers, trying to make a joke of it, to see if I could extricate the *princess* from her momentary lapse. Was there something theatrical in her attitude, or were we on the verge of another episode like the one in Berlin? The referee had to intervene.

"Miss Mass?"

Only then did she slowly assume her position behind the right rectangle and crouch to receive the American's serve. She did so with the mischievousness I had come to know. Love-fifteen, said the referee.

"Welcome, Doctor," said the Countess with relief. "Where have you been?"

"In my room. I had a terrible night."

"Doing what?"

Along with the crowd, I applauded Sophie's second point. Now the winds were blowing in her favor. Nothing pleases a tennis fan as much as stimulating a flagging player with his cheers.

"Thinking."

Diana handed me a brown vial and indicated with her jaw for me to read the label. They were highly potent sleeping pills.

"Last night I had to give these to my daughter so the poor thing could sleep. She was irritable, desperate, crazy."

"My God! Why didn't you call me?"

Together we applauded for Sophie's game.

"That's the problem, Doctor. Last night the cure would have been worse than the illness."

"I don't understand."

"I have the impression that Sophie is in love with you, Doctor."

"I would be delighted to enjoy this final without having to hear inanities, Countess von Mass."

"In love and not Platonically, if you get my drift."

"Fortunately, I don't, Madame."

"Last night she wanted to go and knock on your door. I stopped her by locking her in my room. Finally, she fell asleep in my bed."

"Surely that is just your perception of things."

"I warned you once, Doctor Papst, and now more than ever I admonish you to heed me. Keep your profession separate from your emotional life."

"That is exactly what I am doing," I shouted, my words miraculously silenced by the audience that celebrated Sophie's tying game. Diana fingered the heroic button of her blouse, opened it, closed it, opened it again.

"If you have urgent desires, Doctor ... Paris is full of beautiful women."

"I ask you to be understanding. I am a married man."

"Married, but not in love."

"Beg your pardon?"

"I suspect you are more in love with Baron von Bamberg's

money than you are with your wife."

For a moment I had to take my eyes away from the match in order to look angrily at the mother.

"Countess: this is an unfair match. I am tossing paper wads at you and you reply with neutron bombs."

I made to stand up, but she sat me back down on the bench with virile vigor.

"You know that if you leave Sophie will lose."

"What do you want me to do then?"

"Stay with us until London at least. But I warn you that if you get involved with her I'll tear out your eyes and toss them to the pigs."

"In that case I request that you use the prize money to buy me a seeing-eye dog."

"A dog and a white cane, Doctor!"

Contrary to all predictions, Sophie won the match in two sets, and in the din of the merrymaking, she and her mother lost sight of me. A couple of photographers who, two days before, had begged me to pose with the starlet now greeted me with adolescent informality, not stopping to watch me walk back to the hotel as I treaded on chestnuts fallen from the trees. I was sad. A feeling unknown to me in Berlin but one that Paris brought on, despite all its splendor. It was as if Sophie's success hurt me. As if the almost knavish beauty with which she crowned the tournament were the grandiose beginning of an end. I walked slowly and with a smile that contradicted the irregularity of my heartbeat. At a moment like this, maestro Milosz could have conjured up a poem. Because what is great poetry if not feeling nostalgia for what you have? Even the English have nostalgia for what is lost; but nostalgia for what is still there, only poets feel that. It is not arrogance to suggest that my feeling was *poetic*, even though I did not go in search of metaphors, images, hyperbatons, or allegories to express it. I left that frantic task exclusively to my young rival. The only thing I could say at that moment was that being close to Sophie had made me feel alive. And that is the only dose of garlic I will allow myself.

In my room the phone was ringing. Shaded by melancholy, the tone sounded more strident than usual. Many a time I had let the contraption ring, my hand poised over the receiver, suffering the infantile cowardice of my evasive behavior. In this twilight state of mind a certain degree of maturity is called for. I answered.

"Raymond?"

"Yes."

"This is Mollenhauer speaking."

"Herbert!"

"I'm calling you because, as your colleague and friend, it is my duty to warn you that your wife and your father-in-law have just boarded a plane for Paris."

"What do they want?"

"They don't agree about what they want. The Baron wants to see you turned into a corpse and your wife wants you dead."

"What should I do now?"

"I don't know. But since I doubt you'll find German juridical texts in France, I took the trouble of searching through the penal code for the pertinent clauses. Listen carefully. I'll read from the *Strafgesetzbuch*, Article 182: '*Seduction.* 1.) He who seduces a girl younger than sixteen years of age in order to effect an act of carnal knowledge shall be sentenced to one year in prison, or a fine, or both. 2.) The process shall be initiated only at the petition of the complainant. The actions denounced shall not be subject to investigation if the alleged perpetrator marries the seduced party. 3.) Only in the case of a perpetrator who at the time of the incident has not reached twenty years of age may the court refrain from applying the punishment prescribed by law.'"

"You're a great friend, Herbert."

"At your service."

I went down to the bar to clear my head with a double shot of thirty-year-old malt whiskey. From the airport to the Ritz my father-in-law and Ana would take at least forty-five minutes. I had to be realistic. The first sip of that elixir produced an explosive clarity. There was really only one choice: to check out, pack my bags at once, take a cab to the airport, and fly off in the same Air France liner in which my family would be landing. If the objective of their trip was to convince me to go home, I myself would have done so without being asked and would come up looking pure as driven snow from their standpoint. Better still, upon not finding my wife in Berlin, I would be the one who called Paris and made a fuss. One of my father-in-law's clichés was custom-made for the situation: the best defense is a good offense. I savored the last drop of my thirty-year-old nectar and played with the little ice cube, still impregnated with that delicacy, by tossing it from one side of my mouth to the other. I then thought it would be a shame not to celebrate my tragic decision with a new dose of the same liquor in the same glass but with a new ice cube. Having ordered another drink, with glass in holster and ice cube tinkling to a Brazilian rhythm, I pressed the elevator button. No matter how much I would play the ostrich with my father-in-law and wife, I could not neglect my duties as a physician and a gentleman.

Her door was open. Throughout the room were strewn formal gowns, athletic outfits, underwear, slippers, jewels, shoes, books, and makeup. Hearing running water, I assumed she must be in the bathroom. I headed in that direction, careful not to step on the items spread out on the floor.

I called her name but, with the shower pounding violently on the back of her neck, she did not hear me . The faucet had a pressure valve, and she submitted to the water's impact with her head down and her eyes closed. Only once, in my office, had I had Sophie's nude back before me. On that occasion I had refused to see her body, opting not to allow myself to feel what I really felt. My medical colleagues are very familiar with this neutralizing technique we use when faced with the nudity of an attractive patient. But now, seeing her shine amidst the violent water that was rushing over her skin, made of intimacy and smoothed by a high spiritual tension, I contemplated her without respite.

"Raymond Papst! How many whiskeys did it take for you to decide to come into my room?" she said upon discovering me.

Only then did I notice I had brought the glass with me. I made the ice cubes clink again, happy that Sophie accepted my presence in the bathroom so naturally.

"Just two. But each one was thirty years old."

She put her forehead next to the spout and let the stream hit hard on her cheekbones.

"What are you going to wear to the awards ceremony?"

"I'm not staying for the ceremony, Sophie. I've come to say good-bye."

She slapped the air—that gesture with which the Germans dismiss someone who speaks nonsense.

"You can't go anywhere until they give me the trophy. We won, my love."

"'We won, my love.' Let's forget about the second part of that sentence and discuss the first. *You* won. I am about to lose everything, my little one."

"*You* and *I* won. If you hadn't been with me, I would have lost. Now we'll take the plane to win Wimbledon."

"You'll need a few more years to do that. Not even the most precocious tennis players have won before turning eighteen."

"I'll be the exception. Hand me a towel."

I drank the rest of the liquor, put the glass on the sink, and took the soft lilac towel, wide as a sail. Sophie grabbed it by a corner, gestured for me to open it, and between us we held it taut. With the stream of water still pouring over her shoulders, she began to pull the towel toward her, drawing me slowly into the game. When I was a couple of centimeters from her, without giving me time to react, she wrapped me in the fabric, pinning me, and with a sudden movement she pulled me, fully dressed, toward her nude body in the shower, soaking me instantly from my eyebrows to my shirt. Even though I struggled to free myself, Sophie seemed to draw new vigor from her laughter, and she was able to hold me prisoner in the towel. There came a time when I could resist no longer and I simply let my arms fall, with patient ire letting the water run its course and seep into my pants, socks, shoes. That was the moment when, with a theatrical gesture, she let go of the towel that imprisoned me and, enjoying seeing me drip, as if in a 1930s comedy one might see at a matinee in the neighborhood moviehouse, she leaned against the tiled walls, covering her mouth to hide her false guilt. I gave her a stern glance and left the room.

*   *   *

I was leaving behind me a wake of liquid that reminded me of films in which the criminal, suffering from a gunshot wound, bleeds to death in the arms of his beloved. Even the impassive Ritz bellboys, practiced in the art of inexpressiveness, could not help but turn their heads as I passed and observe with stupefaction the fluid traces of my crime on the rugs. As I turned the key I realized the door was already unlocked. I opened it, and I think the spectacle that presented itself to my eyes must have knocked me off balance. Majestic and seigniorial, with one hand poised on the silken armchair embroidered with motifs of *L'Age de la Raison*, and the other resting on the hilt of his cane-scepter—a creation of Cartier on which the serpent of Epidaurus, the symbol of medicine, coils itself around a mandrake wrought in gold—was my father-in-law.

Seated in the frame of the same window that, the night before, had been shattered by Sophie's compulsive flashes, and with an expression that gave the lie to the usual dignity with which she forgave my stupid trespasses, was Ana, dressed in a tailored tweed executive suit and swinging her coarse leather purse as if it were the pendulum of a clock approaching the fatal hour.

Contrite, I lowered my head and raised my eyes.

"The tribunal assembled in plenary session," I said.

Upon receiving not the slightest smile in reply, I opted to use my tongue before my mind could begin to function. This is the Boston method for distracting the foe's attention away from the *corpus delicti* and toward the verbal bluster.

My wife gestured with her chin toward the bed.

"I've already packed your suitcase. We're flying back to Berlin right now."

In fact, the bag had been neatly closed and on top of it lay my raincoat and the book of poems by Milosz. The *armoire* doors, wide open, revealed their empty compartments. Devastated by Hurricane Ana.

My father-in-law harrumphed in anticipation of a pronouncement. A sure signal that the voice of experience would speak and that he wanted to clear the way of idle chatter.

"Raymond," he said. "Are you feeling all right?"

With what I took to be perfect ingenuousness, I looked into his amazed eyes.

"Me? Terrific, Baron!"

"Do you realize you are soaked from head to stockinged toe and that you are dripping water like a faucet?"

I looked at the tip of my shoes, then I bent one foot and observed my heel for a few seconds.

"Curious," I said.

Before formulating her next sentence, Ana looked outside where a perfectly blue day was taking shape, as if that sky had never known a cloud.

"How did you get so wet?" she asked.

At that moment I would have given anything for the hint of a smile from my mundane father-in-law or a wink of those marvelous green lightning bolts of Ana's. But both remained in funereal silence, the acid expressions on their faces dissolving not one whit.

"Ana, I'll wait for you downstairs in the car!" said the Baron acridly.

He left doing a pirouette with his cane, without conceding me so much as the mercy of a glance. Ana had uncrossed her legs and was stroking her chin.

"Now let's talk in earnest. What's going on with you?" Ana asked.

In the intelligence of her expression, the sweetness of her gesture, the beauty of her features, the elegance of her movements, I knew that the truth I had to speak in homage and respect to such a marvelous person represented utter folly.

"I'm in love with Sophie Mass."

Good-naturedly, she ran an affectionate finger along the ridge of my nose and, upon reaching the fleshy end, gave it a little flick with her nail.

"You're confusing love with admiration. I still have a photo of Robert Redford in my study. Put on something dry and let's return to Berlin."

She pressed the metalic lock on the suitcase and the lid sprang open.

"And what will I do in Berlin?"

"The same as always."

"Oh, no. Change my medication. For once in my life I have to doff my formal attire and let my emotions flow. Life is something else, not the good fortune we have."

At this text of mine, Ana grabbed her handbag from the window sill and slung it over her shoulder with a definitive gesture.

"If you allow me to remind you I am a lawyer, I can affirm from personal experience that the seduction of a minor is punishable by incarceration in every civilized country. Including France!"

"And what should I do?"

"I imagine, clear your head. But I'm not willing to endure the ridiculous spectacle of seeing how things turn out for you in the end. If you don't climb into the car to return to Berlin this instant, don't bother trying it later. Good-bye, Raymond."

Raymond Papst, I said to myself, if within the next minute you don't climb into your father-in-law's limousine, even if you're as soaked as a shipwrecked sailor, in the light of Ana's unequivocal ultimatum you may award yourself the title of Grand Cretin.

The phone rang.

"Raymond? It's Sophie!"

As undeniable proof that I had already begun to exercise the duties pertaining to the title with which I had just dubbed myself, instead of letting flow a whole verbal slurry the princess ought to hear once and for all, I said with polite distance:

"Yes?"

"You should know that the car with your wife and father-in-law has just left."

"Thanks for the information."

"Raymond?"

"What?"

"I want to thank you for everything you've done for me."

To say "you're welcome" would have been too bitter a pill for me to swallow. I simply replaced the receiver on its hook and then caressed its white back as if trying to erase the fingerprints of a delinquent. All of a sudden the room seemed broader and more empty. What did I have going for me now? What the febrile Pablo

Braganza had prognosticated: nothing. Nothing, *niente, nichts, nada*, nothing of nothing, *rien de rien*. I got undressed and, as if choreographing my existential situation, walked about the room again, repeating the same arguments and self-reproaches as usual, without managing to clear my mind but with an anguish that left my throat dry.

One more minute of solitude and I'd surely suffer a thrombosis. *Ergo*: father-in-law's tux, Harvard bow tie, Italian shoes, Ana's cufflinks, thirty-year-old double whiskey, and departure for the awards ceremony.

*   *   *

With the TV cameras and photographers teeming in the space between the first row and the celebrities' platform, it was not possible to see the details of the ceremony. Calm with the certainty of belonging to a star's inner circle, I sank down into the padded seat while everyone else stood on tiptoes trying to snare something. There, amidst the fuss, I wondered how long Sophie could go on without deteriorating, without turning into a machine for smashes, trophies, checks, and fans. What caused my jaded perspective? Not a cowardly paternalistic attitude, but something that derived from Sophie Mass herself, something I could define as a *touch of absence*.

In that *touch of absence*, whatever it means, I felt myself to be her accomplice. It was a common ground I wanted to explore with the intuition that there I would find truth, beauty, excitement, revelations. My mind was not confused to the extent of denying that gambling everything on something so intangible as a *touch of absence* was total idiocy. But that sensation alone justified all the risks where Sophie was concerned. That little bit she gave me was the synopsis of something glorious; but the fragment that connected with a hypothetical whole was at the same time self-sufficient. I *could not* leave Sophie.

Entangled in those ratiocinations, I closed my eyes, wrapping myself in the murmurs of her victory, the clicks of the cameras, the shouts of the photographers asking for another pose, the distant laughter in response to venomous jokes, the orchestra tuning up to play at any moment. That's why I didn't see Sophie arrive at my side. On other occasions she had privileged me with her presence when everyone was clamoring for her, and we had spent hours together, without exchanging more than a few words, both of us a bit lost at the threshold of the undefinable. But that she should appear now, and that I should awake to the impulse of her voice and witness her almost unreal image, with the silver trophy in her right hand, a mountain of multicolored flowers in her left, and her cheeks flushed to a violent scarlet, was an honor that left me breathless. I jumped to my feet with the agility of a boxer who has been knocked to the canvas for the count of ten, and I tried to etch that picture for my old age, as a consolation before death: Sophie the queen, princess, crown, laurel, angel, ecstasy, *before* me, *for* me.

Then the girl did the spontaneous, the unusual, obeying what some might call impulse, but what here was simply madness: like a bride offering her bouquet to the ladies in waiting, she ostentatiously threw that orgy of flowers to the heavens, and with her free arm she enveloped me, taking the nape of my neck in her hand. With a strength I could not resist, she brought my mouth to her lips and gave me a long kiss in front of a public that apprehended the scandalous nature of the act and the apathetic tone the detail lent to the tournament's conclusion.

Upon removing her tongue from my mouth, she looked at me with such solemn depth that the reproach I normally should have issued struck me as shameful cowardice. Sensing I was courting disaster, and that this was almost certainly the golden colophon with which Sophie was sealing our relationship, I sustained her glance with that same dignity, that same silence. At that instant I thought, I repeat, *I thought* we were both at the core of that *touch of absence*, and that they could now lower the curtain on us at that moment of plenitude.

Inevitably, Countess von Mass came at me with a threatening gesture and had me follow her while the photographers, surprised by the kiss, were begging Sophie to repeat it and the rest of the journalists were showing an opportunistic interest in me. I paid their questions no heed and followed the Countess toward the park that surrounded the locale, while she went about dispersing the curiosity seekers with cutting phrases. For a few minutes I didn't know where she was leading me, and I suppose she, too, was wondering where to start. When we arrived at a fountain where cute little angels were urinating beneath their prominent bellies, Diana stopped and, without according me even the shadow of a glance, said:

"Sophie has an intelligence and a talent that don't seem to fit in her body."

"Exactly," I agreed.

"And then one begins to think what else could fit in that body, right?"

I clapped my palms together angrily, not caring a hoot that people were coming over to look. I, who had been a *prima ballerina* of delicacy on the high wire, took a pie of that size in the face, like in a Marx Brothers' farce.

"Bravo, Madame!" I whispered to her, clenching my teeth. "As the last dialogue we will have in our lives, this one strikes me as brilliant and consequential. The touch of vulgarity lends to my suffering a certain vitality that was heretofore missing from this comedy in which you have ensnared me. I wish you every success in Wimbledon."

I left with a firm and sustained stride, and after a couple of minutes I felt an urge to run. So I crossed the park among professional joggers who contemplated in stupefaction how someone carried out their ritual attired in a tuxedo and patent-leather slippers.

My suitcase lay on the bed, just as Ana had left it. All I had to do was replace the tux, collect a bundle of dirty clothes, insert Milosz's vainly concupiscent book along with the Harvard butterfly, and take immediate flight. As I removed the formal jacket I could perceive Sophie's aroma on the padded shoulder.

She wore no perfume, but her extreme youth nonetheless emanated a certain unmistakable fragrance. I confess I lay back on the bed—in the darkness, embracing the jacket, my mouth sunk into the fabric—possessed of a melancholy the likes of which I knew only from sentimental pulp novels.

At that moment Sophie Mass entered my room.

$$*\qquad*\qquad*$$

She came slowly toward my bed and sat at the head with the aplomb of someone visiting a sick friend on a Sunday afternoon at a sultry hospital in the provinces.

"So you're leaving, Raymond Papst?" she said so low that if I had not been in a state of sensory hyperstimulation, I could not have heard her. I thought it best not to comment. "Why are you going?"

I ran my hand over my cheek, relieved at having that stubble of a few hours' growth through which to discharge my nervous energy.

"Raymond, why don't you answer?"

There were so many reasons to give her. Except that every word seemed to me stale before pronouncing it. The film was over.

"Look at me."

"Why have you come?"

"I wanted to thank you for all you've done for me."

"That's all right."

"I beg you to forgive me for what I've done."

"What are you referring to?"

"The kiss in front of everybody."

"Something else?"

She brought her right hand forward and placed the edge of her fingernails over my upper lip.

"I want to sleep with you."

I raised my jaw a little so her fingers now rested on my lower lip. With a vestige of my tongue I devoutly moistened her fingertips.

"Raymond?"

"No."

"Who would know?"

"*I* would know and that's enough. I'm fifty-two years old, Sophie. And at that age one is responsible for what one does. Or for what one doesn't do," I concluded dispiritedly.

"And I'm sixteen."

"Fifteen."

"In a month I'll be sixteen. You can't ask me at my age to share your sense of responsibility."

At that instant I took her index finger and bit it very gently. I was moved by the gravity with which she had discussed her age, so typical of children, for whom each extra year is a trophy. Or was she aware that, with respect to the penal code, between fifteen and sixteen lay an abyss?

"You have no compassion, young lady," I said.

I detest revealing that I was touched. My eyes were moist with tears, something Sophie learned of when she ran her fingers across my eyelids. Without wanting to mitigate my responsibility, I have to evoke the following paradox. When her lips replaced her fingers on my forehead, I felt as if we had switched roles: *she* was the sage artisan who returned peace to me by inspiring me with her breath and running her tongue over my coarse cheek. *She* was the experienced woman and I the pacified child, longing for her tenderness. I was turning into an adolescent as Sophie slowly kissed my chest, to the sway of her sweet nose circulating among my chest hairs, to the touch of her chin marauding my navel, to the heat of her tongue that kept hinting at crossing the border of my waistline.

At that moment, the last trace of a sense of accountability had me brake the course of her lips by raising a hand and placing it as a blunt barrier in front of her mouth. But right away I was fascinated by the placid vigor with which she brushed my fingers aside, rested them on top of the sheet, and continued her itinerary until reaching her goal, immersing me in a swoon of pleasure. I had no more words with which to stop her when she anointed with her saliva the head of my sexual organ and, leaning over it, rolled back with her little fingers the skin that covered it to expose my flesh to her tongue.

Afraid that my ecstasy, incubated in different cities and during days and nights of insomnia, would explode brutally in the girl's mouth, I touched her jaw, brought her lips to my mouth, and kissed them intensely, tasting on them the flavor of my own skin. I put her on her back, her chestnut hair spilling over the pillow and the tip of her naughty tongue peering out through the gap between her lips, swollen with excitement. But as soon as the girl understood that I would be mounting her to penetrate her, she seemed to be shaken by an unforeseen panic. She covered her pubis with her hand and writhed, avoiding the kiss with which I advanced toward her mouth. I made an effort to remove her hand from her belly, imagining its placement was only a strategem to magnify my delight, but she protected herself by contracting her thighs.

I opened the buttons of her white silk blouse and slid my fingers over her little breasts, dizzy from the pleasure of feeling them swelling, full of sex and youth.

I took her hand and put it firmly over my sex. I searched for her eyes in order to ask her imperiously to yield. She caressed the length of the surface of my organ and brought her same hand to her nose to breathe deeply of its odor.

Sophie jumped from the bed, and standing on the rug she unfastened her skirt, which she placidly slid to her feet. Sinking her fingernails into the elastic of her panties, she untangled them from between her legs, tossing them in two precise movements over the tapestry. Then she backed toward the wall and slid along it, her head very close to the light switch. Then she arched her abdomen and, stretching out her arm, begged me to go to her. I hesitated, between anger and excitement. I was both so deeply humiliated and at the same time so febrile that I preferred to follow her body's infallible signals. I went toward her with the clear purpose of entering her. Since the beginning of time, that has been the meaning of *to sleep with someone*, and that is what the girl had proposed to me when she said *I want to sleep with you*. I was not about to be detoured in the zigzags of possible euphemisms. I rudely pressed with my sex against her pubis, only to receive the one response that was capable of sending me straight to the realm of anguish: she placed both hands on top of my head and pressed down in a clear signal for me to kneel.

Filled with humiliation, I sank my tongue into her vagina. While the script was being carried out according to the prescribed lyrical Spanish outpourings—which now, contrasted with reality, I could take as exercises in naturalistic realism—and while Sophie's body—aided by my absolute concentration on her most intimate skin—neared climax, my mouth was braked by a fit of dignity. I was functioning like a marionette, as if a prompter or some rubicund angel with eyes half-closed by infirmity were dictating every movement.

I suspended my actions just when she was about to take off, and departing from the memorized script I lifted little Sophie by the buttocks, deposited her in *blitzkrieg* fashion back on the good old bed, and before she could reinitiate her complicated defense patterns, I inserted myself into her without concern for finery. If willfulness clouded my judgment, if folly made me blind and deaf to her pain, ecstasy plunged me into the singular perception of my bliss.

*   *   *

"Doctor Papst!"

An obese man wearing a raincoat stood next to my bed, an unlit cigarette in his mouth, a camera dangling over his chest, a honeyed smile stretched from one end of his mouth to the other. At my side slept Sophie, one arm beneath the pillow, covered up only to her waist. With an abrupt gesture I covered her breasts.

"Who are you?"

"Alain Bracourt, journalist."

"What are you doing in my room?"

"Pictures."

"Who gave you the authority to enter?"

"My inspiration."

He walked with no embarrassment toward the window to open the thick curtain and expose our bodies to the golden morning light.

I theatrically grabbed the telephone, but the photographer remained undaunted.

"I'll call the police. What you're doing is an impertinence and a crime."

With my upbraidings, Sophie awoke and looked hazily, almost smiling, at the large stranger, who shot off more than ten pictures in a row.

"When it comes to crimes, I risk a fine. You, a year in jail, at least."

"I can do without the insolence. Sophie and I are going to be married."

Bracourt extracted the unlit cigarette from the left corner of his mouth and made as if to knock off an imaginary ash by feigning to tap it at the height of his eyes.

"Congratulations. A bit of news that will calm our readers' sense of moral outrage. But until the wedding is *executed*— begging your pardon for the police terminology—we have a scandal that will arouse interest beyond the borders of France."

"What's going on, Raymond?" asked Sophie with a yawn.

"Cover yourself, please," I called.

"If I understand your intentions, sir, we have here a case of blackmail, right?"

Bracourt took a carefree swipe at the air.

"It looks like blackmail, but it isn't really," he said, sitting insolently on the edge of the Ritz's fragile rococo easy chair, giving the appearance of utter calm. "In the old days, blackmail used to work because it was much more lucrative to extort money from a person than to publish the picture in the newspapers. Today, with the proliferation of electronic media, all you have to do is turn the material in question over to an agent and you get almost as much as you would with blackmail, but with none of the legal risks. The material is reproduced by the wire services in a variety of countries, is picked up by TV, etc. And the way to make good money is to let the story unfold gradually. You reveal a titillating tidbit to the public at first. If the story catches on, all the media come after you with interesting offers to buy the supporting documentation. Do you follow me, Doctor Papst?"

I looked despondently at Sophie, who smiled at me innocently, and then I turned back toward the photographer.

"Then we're screwed!"

Bracourt launched a laugh proportional to the size of his

body and vigorously slapped his thighs as if witnessing a schoolboy's prank.

"You screwed, Doctor Papst? How can you say that while in the arms of that *princess*? A young lady with whom half the Western world would like to enjoy the intimacy she grants you? You're not screwed, Professor! You are at the peak of glory, the apex of fame, stardom! And my modest photographs are only going to contribute to your career. The one who's screwed is me, Doctor Papst, doing this miserable job for a few crummy francs, with my health deteriorating."

"What's the matter, my man?" I said, suddenly professional, hoping to soften his heart with science.

"High blood pressure and overweight, Doctor."

"How much do you weigh?"

"I can't get below 265."

"And your blood pressure?"

"It won't go below 140."

"But that's very good!"

"It's the *minimum* that won't go below 140, Doctor."

"Are you taking pills?"

"Half a vial of *Beloc* per day."

"And?"

"Well, that's what keeps my pressure from going higher, according to my doctor."

He stood up and, with a philosophical air, rubbed his neck for a minute.

"You have a great racket, Doctor Papst! Your story will resound far beyond the provincial borders of Paris. You're an American, aren't you?"

"Bostonian."

"Money there is worth something. Here the franc is only good for playing *Monopoly*."

I looked at him inquiringly to see whether, behind the façade, he still wanted to play the card of blackmail.

"How much?" I asked cautiously.

The man closed his leather camera case, almost sadly.

"Don't offend me, please."

"What should I do? Despite all your persuasive arguments, the publication of this story will ruin us."

"Why, Raymond?" asked Sophie.

"I can't discuss it now in front of this individual."

Bracourt removed the unlit cigarette from his mouth, went over to the ashtray, and crushed it as if he had just finished smoking it.

"My doctor unconditionally forbids me to use tobacco. Now I smoke like this, nothing but play acting," he said with melancholy.

"I warn you, Mr. Bracourt. If you publish one of those pictures, I'm going to sue you for so much that when you receive the notification your heart is going to explode like a grenade."

"Aha! So that's your idea of professional ethics, Doctor. Give your patients heart attacks?"

"You're no patient of mine, sir. You are a criminal!"

"Which of the two of us is the criminal is something the justice system will have to decide."

"Is it or is it not a crime to enter someone else's room and take photos without his consent?"

"In principle, yes. But in practice the French judges look the other way when it has to do with public figures. For example, in an encounter before the court, in my case the judges would have to take into account the extenuating circumstances."

"What extenuating circumstances?"

"That there was no attempt on your part to keep your love story covered. The kiss the young lady gave you on the mouth last night in full view of everyone gave away the secret. No one obliged you to neck in public, did they?"

And he emphatically extracted a copy of *France Soir* from his pocket and unfolded the headlines. There were two pictures, each the size of a sheet of manuscript paper. The first of the trophy, amidst a suspect floral arrangement, and the other of the historic kiss, in which one could see in the extreme foreground the consternation of Countess von Mass.

"I regret the inconvenience, Doctor Papst, but I've made my career as a journalist by being faithful to the motto 'You can't make an omelette without breaking eggs.' Good bye, sir. *Aufwiedersehen, Fraulein.*"

"*Aufwiedersehen*," answered Sophie with one of those smiles that came straight from her soul.

I was about to sigh deeply, to try to relax my tensed muscles, when, through the same doorway through which the journalist Alain Bracourt had left, there entered Countess Diana von Mass.

The girl hopped into the dress, slipped into her shoes on the way toward the door, and, once at the threshold, threw me a kiss, anointing two fingers together over her lips.

Diana von Mass went over to the window and grasped the curtain as if she were wringing a towel. Suddenly she turned her body and confronted me with a voice as lofty as her posture.

"What do you have to say to me now, Doctor Papst?"

"Good morning, Mother-in-law," I essayed with a roguish grin.

"This is no joking matter."

I indicated my immodest body, hardly covered by the sheet, and I threw my arms up in anguish.

"What do you expect me to do? For the past hour all sorts of people have been entering this room without permission, not even giving me a chance to get dressed. I feel as though I'm acting in some ridiculous Italian farce."

The Countess turned her back with a haughty movement.

"Get dressed."

I grabbed my things and stuffed myself into them with the utmost haste. After putting on my socks, I decided to delay tying my shoelaces, since I sensed I'd need something with which to fill the fatal silences that were to come. The Countess took to pacing resolutely, like a wild beast, from one end of the room to the other.

"You know that for most of my life I have regretted having a child out of wedlock."

"I know, Countess."

By this time I had tied and untied my shoelaces three times. I interrupted this operation to study Diana's expression after hearing my words.

"We have to be practical. I know my daughter, and I know she'll throw you out sooner rather than later, leaving you bleeding like a common bottle of ketchup. What matters now is that she win Wimbledon, and evidently you provide her with the erotic stimulation necessary for her to produce optimally on the court."

She moved toward the door and gave me a look that seemed rather like a threatening prophecy.

"The flight to London is tomorrow at noon. Anything else, Doctor Papst?"

"Yes, Madame. If you would be so kind as to pay me my honorarium. I fear Baron von Bamberg has disinherited me by now."

The Countess waved the championship check in the air and said, with the obvious pleasure of speaking about something that did arouse her passion:

"As soon as I cash this monster, you'll have your share."

As soon as Diana had left, I sprang toward the door and double locked it. I wanted to relive the emotions of the night before and celebrate with hours of deep stillness the discovery of love. So many caresses had been frustrated by the turbulence of events! So many words, polished during Sophie's slumber, that I would have wished to murmur in her ear in order to express loquaciously my thanks for the excitement of living with which she had regaled me, and which I was not able to tell her! I walked about the room with the solemnity of one who sets foot in a temple, collecting the simple items that in the morning brilliance truly seemed to be trophies of love: her panties, a long hair on the pillow.

*   *   *

On the plane to London I read the French newspapers. All the papers ran Bracourt's ignominious photos. Only *Le Monde* abstained from printing our half-naked images, but just because that prestigious newspaper never used graphics. On the other hand, it mused ironically about my situation in a little article of ten lines where, in homage to Nabokov, I was referred to as "Mister Lolita." All in all, I should have been grateful for that discretion: the rest of the press oscillated between demanding that I be burned at the stake—on one page they evoked the arduous fate of the maid of Orleans—and celebrating me as an international Don Juan, a sort of hybrid between Christiaan Barnard and Robert Redford.

The pictures were more ridiculous than the situation in which they had been taken. As an actor in a drama, one is so immersed in the process that it is impossible to imagine how farcical everything looks from a distance. In the images, thanks to Monsieur Bracourt's diabolical artistry, I appear with the face of a hoary satyr, my chest uncovered, shouting at the journalist to desist from shooting us. That is the kindest one. In the other one I shield my face from the flashes as if I were a criminal. Any court of law in the world that saw those documents would sentence me to life in prison. And Sophie—always ingenuous, fresh, superior—in each image grants the scoundrel a smile of such candor that in contrast my slavering fangs resemble those of a voluptuous and sanguinary beast, a sort of wolf that had just gobbled down the grandmother for breakfast and now was about to serve itself the innocent tennis player for dessert.

I should not omit the epithets with which I was branded in the captions, since they have greatly influenced public opinion: "The American Satyr," "The Corrupting Physician." Another one simply took recourse to a dictionary of synonyms: "Papst: concupiscent, horny, incontinent, lascivious, lewd, libidinous, lubricious, lustful, unbridled, wanton." The ultra-rightist scandal sheet indulged in a play on words with my surname: "No Papal pardon for Papst."

Soaring over the English Channel I found two consolations. In their order of importance: as if she had guessed my suffering, Sophie touched my hand and delicately kissed my wrist. The second source of relief was having left France behind, where the Parisians no longer reacted complicitously to the ecstasies of love, saying "Ooh, la, la," as in the Maurice Chevalier films of my infancy, but rather seemed intent on reestablishing the ever-popular guillotine for lovers.

But the reporters, their sanguine instincts primed by the French press, were in rare form at the airport. I omit the most vulgar gaffes in order to allow the polite questions to stand out.

(To Sophie): "What would you do if you became pregnant by Doctor Papst?"

(To Sophie): "How thick is your racket handle?"

(To Countess von Mass): "A *ménage à trois*?"

(To me): "Would you like it if this happened to your daughter?"

(To Sophie): "How was Doctor Papst's performance on your honeymoon in Paris?"

I interrupt this list to report that, despite all my admonitions not to go into discussions about our private life, Sophie answered, arrogantly tossing her hair back:

"Fantastic!"

Which brought a storm of flashes to my face, just at the instant when I could not repress my indignation at her *faux pas*, shouting:

"Shut up, for mercy's sake."

That was the moment when, for the first time, the girl took from her infinite arsenal of expressions haughtiness, inflamed wrath, rebelliousness, a surly grimace, and, I admit with pain, scorn:

"You shut up, you idiot. I'm not your daughter and don't have to take orders from you."

Since we had barked at each other in German, the photographers remained dumbstruck, until one of them asked an old man with a wily face who was taking notes:

"What did she say?"

"'I may look like your daughter, but I'm not her,'" translated the bounder, causing laughter that to this day resounds in my eardrums.

To get to the hotel we divided ourselves between two vehicles. Countess von Mass went with a most delicate reporter from *The Times*, who in the airport had had the gentility to whisper in my ear the following sentence of consolation: "Even if you liked to fornicate with canaries, it's not my business. *The Times* will speak only of tennis." Of course, a fellow like that would have absolved me, but in emphasizing his tolerance he was only insinuating to me that his behavior was the exception and not the rule.

In the other vehicle were Sophie, myself, and the entrepreneur Forbes, who drove proferring merry honks of the horn to pedestrians and drivers alike. Affected by the vulgarity we had just suffered through, I could not control myself and, in front of Forbes, assailed Sophie:

"How can you be so stupid as to answer those hyenas' questions?"

"I speak to whomever I wish."

"Doesn't my case matter to you?"

"Your case?"

"My little one, don't you realize we are mired in a scandal?"

"That's your problem."

"My problem?"

"Don't bum me out by ordering me around."

"So you couldn't care less about my ruin?"

"What do I know about that!"

"When we reach the hotel I'm leaving."

"*Bon voyage!*"

"As soon as we get there you run straight to our room without talking to anyone and close yourself in there until I tell you otherwise."

"Doctor Papst. When we reach the hotel, Sophie has to stay for half an hour in the lobby. The bulk of the reporters are waiting for her there," said Forbes.

"What about the ones at the airport?"

"Photographers!"

"I love pictures," Sophie exclaimed, turning her other cheek to the wind.

"Miss Mass is right. One must attend to the press."

"No, Mister Forbes. The press is *kaput*!"

"I don't understand your attitude, Doctor Papst. The boys are excited about Sophie's match. We're charging twice the normal admission price, and with a little publicity we'll sell out the entire stadium."

"It's not tennis you're interested in; it's scandal."

"In this atmosphere it is customary to add a little sauce to the meal."

"But Mr. Forbes! Sophie is a tennis player, not a striptease artist."

"That's the marvel of it! A girl who combines with her talent that eroticism, that sensuality." He let out the guffaw of a good ol' boy in a small town bar. "But, why am I telling you? You know her more intimately."

"What do you mean by that, you swine?"

"Doctor Papst, we are in London, a place of which a humanist like Erasmus of Rotterdam said: 'A city in which I would stay until the end of my days, if I could!'"

"Mr. Forbes, the match is cancelled."

"If you call off the match Sophie's fans will lynch you. And if you survived the lynching my lawyers would make sure you languished in jail."

"Remember I am a doctor and that there is an irrefutable argument: Sophie is ill!"

The girl leaned forward over the impresario's earlobe and said softly, but just loudly enough for me to hear:

"Don't worry, Mr. Forbes. I make the decisions about my matches."

The man placed a hand on Sophie's cheek and gave it the pat of a doddering grandfather.

"Talented, pretty, and smart."

And he celebrated his conclusions with a new concert of horn beeps.

"This very night I return to Berlin," I said.

"Berlin," said Sophie, with irony.

"Berlin," said I, with conviction.

*   *   *

In the hotel lobby I shoved my way through the newspaper people and picked up, in a supremely private ceremony, the keys to our rooms. It was Forbes's brainchild that Sophie and I should sleep sufficiently apart so as not to offend the Countess's, the hotel's, and the press's sense of morality, but at the same time sufficiently close so that we could share the same bed and so that the reporters could speculate sagaciously on that proximity. The strategem consisted of assigning me room 500, which communicated through an internal door with 501, to be occupied by Sophie. Grasping the key as if it were a machine gun I crossed the lobby, where journalists and amateurs alike gloated over the ingenuousness of my love.

In the room I desperately opened doors, windows, and I tore off my clothes, scattering them randomly. Between 501 and 500 I went about venting my rage with long strides and punches in the air that were aimed metaphorically at Forbes, the journalists, Bracourt.

I was the scapegoat, the famous fall guy, the punching bag on which everyone practiced their martial arts. With what diplomas had I earned that privilege? "With the diplomas of love"; nice verse for a stupid radio ballad. The world was caving in around us, mainly because of Sophie's impulses and fickleness, and she, unfazed, seemed to enjoy the contact with each brick as it broke our heads.

Ten, twenty minutes passed and she did not come up. I lay down again in the bed in 501. I tossed about for thirty seconds, got up, and fell into mine in 500, ruffling the sheets and my heart. Night fell. Distant bells tolled, and to kill time I tried to tell if some of them belonged to Big Ben. A pigeon alighted on the window sill. We stared at each other for a couple of minutes, until I tried to pet it. It flew away and landed in a tree. A little while later all the birds fled when a fire alarm stirred the air. I went back to her bed and with the palms of my hands I stroked, caressed, the sheets. We would sleep in her room, this time. Surrounded by her dresses, with that fragrance of hers that she imparted to each one of her things. I would hang her three or four hats about the room, and when she was nude in my arms, I would have her don the riding cap that graced her lovely head in the Berlin airport. Why didn't she come?

I went to the adjacent room, moved by the premonition that her arrival was imminent, to look for the silver pail with its bottle of champagne and the exquisite vase whose red roses seemed like a karate chop of sensuality. When I moved it I found an envelope containing a card from *Alexander Forbes, Developer:* "For the lovebirds." A subtle allusion to the fortuitous love story that linked me with the *princess*. But in hard times champagne is the best of companions, and even if it were a gift of the devil himself, I decided I had to give it its due. I ostentatiously shot the cork toward the street, and on serving myself the first glass some of the foam spilled onto the back of my hand, which I licked with my tongue. Where was Sophie?

She had humiliated me in front of the photographers at the airport and had massacred me in front of Forbes. Did she do it in cold blood, to reduce me to the role of a marionette, or was it only one more gesture of her youthful spontaneity?

Damnable, utterly damnable love.

A little girl had me at her complete mercy. She dragged me about. She ridiculed me. She had me jumping from country to country like a grasshopper. She riddled me with love. Why deny it? If scorn were all she were inclined to show me, I would gladly accept it as long as she did not banish me from her side.

I spent three hours, consumed in my own degradation.

Solitude began to smother me.

Uneasiness was beginning to give me chills!

What was Sophie doing at this moment? Where was she?

Thus wounded, I looked at the décor of the room Forbes, in his capacity as go-between, had accorded us, and I tried to see it through his eyes: a tapestry that stretched from one end of the wall to the other with a motif of Swan Lake. A fragile dancer levitated over the waters while swans encircled her with their wings and a slender hunter tensed the bow of his arrow on whose tip, like a flash forward, already hung the bleeding heart at which he pointed. The hotel charged five-star prices, even though its artwork warranted only two. Nonetheless, the artist's ingenuous idea of creating such a strident effect with the arrow was touching.

Sophie was not coming to soothe me.

She was avoiding me.

With the same spontaneity with which she had given me her love, now she was taking it from me. If the first had been unlikely, the second was more than probable. Proof was the berating she give me in full public view: less than a lover, less than a doctor, less than a man, less than a dog.

Were my few authoritarian and paternal words, said only for her good, enough for her to withdraw all her love, like a violent undertow? Was she capable of such extremism? She had told me with her body and her words that she loved me. Then why didn't she come?

A hunch: something had happened to her.

One of her typical pre-tournament impulses. A trip to a *boîte*, the cab collides at a corner, she lies in the hospital. She agonizes.

I showered with cold water and rubbed my body so hard it hurt.

Useless.

This anguish was also love.

I got dressed without paying attention to what I was putting on. Surely the jacket would be full of wrinkles, the pants would be covered with wine stains, the shirt would still have a circle of lipstick from her kiss.

I ran down the stairs while a photographer pursued me shooting off his flashes. I ignored him. I asked the concierge for Sophie.

"She is in her room," he said.

"What number?"

"501."

"That can't be. Don't lie to me."

The employee made a bewildered face. My God! Me, involved in an offense against a poor and sad functionary whom all of a sudden I saw as a son-of-a-bitch hired by Forbes to confound me, to put me off Sophie's trail. I entertained the extravagant idea that my loved one's absence was one of Forbes's tactics. Fearful I might use my authority as her doctor, he had simply kidnapped her and placed her safely out of my clutches in another hotel.

I entered the bar and slumped so pathetically over the table that the waiter served me a double whiskey without even asking me what I wanted. How I must have looked to arouse the sympathetic solidarity of the bartender so early in the evening.

*   *   *

I fixed my gaze on the melancholy fingers of the black pianist. Too bad this wasn't a film set in North Africa where love's misfortune would end when the image on the screen was turned off. The music and the drink dulled my anger and transformed it little by little into sadness. I looked for a mirror to give me the final proof of my destruction. In so doing I spun a bit on the bar stool, and my intuition rather than my eyes seemed to discover Sophie at the table in the farthest corner of the place. The light was very tenuous, and the candelabras emitted a small clarity that confused rather than defined features. I went over to the column next to the pianist and, in a pose I thought discreet, sharpened my focus on that corner.

It was she.

I pressed my fingers over my eyelids and rubbed them as if wishing to erase a hallucination, to unstick a nightmare that clung to them like a tick. Why was she wearing that marvelous dress of light blue velvet with luminous pearls, resembling stars, over her bodice and those fifties-style broad shoulders that made her torso more slender and her movements more sensual? Where had she changed her tennis blouse and the sloppy jeans she had worn during the flight? Why had she chosen a formal evening gown for a simple night in the bar of her own hotel?

One did not have to be an English bloodhound to conclude that a change of clothes requires an intermediate stage during which she was nude!

According to the concierge this change had to have been effected in room 501, a den in which I myself had stalked like a jaguar in heat. Why had I affronted a lowly employee when he indicated to me the room number? I *knew* the false information was not his fault. But wasn't my disproportionate reaction perhaps due to a sardonic glint I perceived, or thought I sensed, in his eyes? I lowered my hands from my eyes and, in a fit of anguish, defenseless as a child, I crammed the fingers of one of my hands into my mouth. And then I could see that Sophie was not alone, nor was she accompanied by a multitude of hangers-on, journalists, or admirers. She was *alone with one man*. And she was listening to this man with mature intensity, as if this expression were appropriate to the fabric of her dress, the severe harmony of the velvet.

I was on the verge of losing my balance.

This too is love, I told myself. This jealousy.

If I wanted to see the face of the *other*—my horror spontaneously named him that—I would have to leave the column and move through the room first toward the left and then forward in order to make out his profile. But I was paralyzed by shame. Rather, I was afraid Sophie would discover me spying on her and revile me even more. Subject me to another public humiliation. I would not move from there. I would wait, diminished and servile, for her to get up. Even if it took hours.

But a minute later, and just when the band was ending a tune with a tremolo, the man who was face-to-face with Sophie turned around to call the waiter by snapping his fingers with the vulgarity of a Yankee sailor.

It was as if ground glass had been thrown into my eyes. The man who was with her was clearly, plainly, undeniably Pablo Braganza.

*   *   *

I have no idea where I got the strength to go toward him; anyway, everything now is more a probable invention of my fantasy than a chronicle of events. Vertigo had taken possession of me, and it would be unfair to demand of a sleepwalker a detailed account of his acts, no matter how tragic they might be. More than actions, it is the frightful dimensions of my pain that I can outline. But with remnants of lucidity and eyewitness reports I was able to piece together this tale, not exact but still plausible.

I may have worn a false smile on my lips when I stopped at their table, but it had to have turned acrid when I observed that her hand rested, with that relaxation that follows moments of intimacy, on his forearm. Upon noticing my presence she brought her hand back toward her hair, buffeting it back regally, and before

I could say what I had in mind, she pulled the rug out from under me.

"Where have you been all this time?" said she, fresh, aggressive, scolding, frigid.

All things considered, it was a sentence less fatal than the one issued by Braganza, who stood up while feigning to clean with his nails some ash on the lapel of his burgundy jacket:

"I told you so, Raymond!"

I am familiar, to the point of horror, with the extant versions of my behavior in the seconds that followed.

The only truth is that, to avoid punching him in the jaw, where his youthful haughtiness and beauty were concentrated, I jammed my hands into my jacket pockets, as if consigning myself to a preventive prison.

I was trembling. They were treating me like a nice little dog that had come wagging its tail, asking to be petted. To have lived that banality disgusts me, but having to evoke it depresses me more. What happened in the next instant certainly is a contrivance of fate. I have no other explanation for all the symmetries and parallelisms, which seem fashioned more by a wizard than by reality. We were at a nightspot in London, as we had been at a nightspot in Berlin before. I was being humiliated in London, as I had been humiliated in Berlin. The cast in Berlin consisted of two adolescents, to wit, Sophie Mass and Pablo Braganza, and one zombie: Raymond Papst. The London crew was comprised of the same characters and the same spirit. Why is it so exotic—so *incredible*, as the lawyers angrily and scornfully repeat in their immoral libel suits—that, convulsed with rage and distress, upon sinking my hands in my pockets I should find in one of them a metallic object that should assume the surprising shape of the high-calibre revolver with which Mr. Braganza had attempted his melodramatic suicide in Berlin?

I didn't even point at him. It was a movement dictated by that damned script, by that road I never should have taken.

I cannot say *I shot* him, for that formulation implies a certain will, a degree of control over one's own faculties, and the decision to convoke them in a plan of aggression. *My hand* squeezed the trigger and the bullet flew. So simple a sentence has cost me so many nights of insomnia to articulate. I cannot take credit for it because its semantics convey a misfortune, but at least it describes, in my opaque physician's language, a truth. I say *my hand* and not *I* because between my awareness and my acts there stretched an abyss.

I awoke with the detonation to see Pablo tumble at my feet. I could not manage to do anything other than to contemplate him from a perplexed distance.

Placing the weapon on the tablecloth like any sort of object—a glass, the ashtray, the pack of cigarettes—I slowly made my way through the onlookers, who in the semi-darkness could not stop me. *I*—who, since violence repulses me, had never held a weapon in my hands—had shot a human being. *I* who in all sincerity had become a doctor in order to cure wounds and not to inflict them. *I* who not even in primary school had observed the healthy custom of engaging in fistfights with the other little boys, accepting instead with burning ears the provocations of their punches, my cheeks wet from the spit with which they punished my cowardice. *I*, a thousand times the dove amidst a pack of wolves, perpetrating a crime!

How was it possible? Every time someone had caused me physical or moral harm, I always went out of my way to look for reasons to justify my enemy's behavior and to doubt with pathological skepticism my own thinking. Did this love for a fifteen-year-old awaken in me the belligerent adolescent I had kept repressed for decades? How could my life in the past few weeks have swerved so that I had actually *shot* the pale and melancholy Pablo Braganza, as if he were some gangster escaped from a movie? No: *My hand squeezed the trigger and the bullet flew.*

*   *   *

It has been charged that, as a doctor, I did not show sufficient concern for the boy who was bleeding on the barroom floor. Witnesses have said I fled from the scene of the crime, revealing a coldness and an indifference incompatible with professional ethics. How can I have fled if I remained in the hotel, in my room, shaken by uncontrollable heart palpitations?

The only thing I desired was for this to lead to a coronary thrombosis.

So massive that it burst my arteries for once and for all.

Sophie didn't love me any more.

With the same compelling spontaneity with which she had presented her love, now she withdrew it. In a matter of minutes, the room the astute Forbes had roguishly decorated for our ceremonies of love was turned into the mausoleum of my agony.

Outside, there was a hallucinatory ocean of noises: conversations between tourists from Texas in the hallway, the echo of shouts from the lobby, the siren of an ambulance muffled by the curtains, the monotonous whine of a vacuum cleaner on the top floor. The siren grew softer and then reappeared, as if it were lost somewhere in London, with that irritating ubiquitousness that alarms can have. My hands were moist, shaken by an uncontrollable current. I went to dry them on my pants, only to realize my thighs, too, were damp.

I went over to the window and pressed my forehead against the glass. The cold contact lasted scarcely seconds. Upon standing upright I noticed a repugnantly shaped stain and erased it with the sleeve of my jacket. I saw the ambulance pull up to the hotel door and the doorman and manager, who shoved their way through the crowd for the medics. The blue light kept spinning noiselessly, and I recalled a lighthouse in Connecticut, when on a night of fog and felicity we would look for the dock with my father's flashlight.

They knocked at the door. Startled, I wiped my hands on the lapels of my jacket.

"It's me," said Sophie.

I went to let her in. If her pallor had always captivated me, now she had an ashen tinge that lent her an unreal quality. I foresaw a horrible scene coming and prepared myself to confront her by marshalling the forces I did not have. Nonetheless, she went with remarkable serenity toward the window and watched what was happening below.

"They're taking him to the hospital," she said with her back to me.

For a second I had the impression I was a spectator to this scene, that I was outside the play, in the safety of my routine, and that the Raymond Papst who now wished against all sanity and with the greatest persistence to go to her and embrace her, to kiss her neck and bite her, was a fifth-rate actor stumbling through my part.

"Sophie," I called, without moving toward her.

Now she did turn around, without losing a tad of her calm.

"Why did you kill him?"

I had to lean against the wall to support myself.

"Is he dead?"

"That's what they're saying."

"Is he dead?"

"I don't know."

"My God! You had to have noticed if he was alive or not."

"It wasn't possible to tell! And the only doctor in the house had *fled*."

"I didn't *flee*."

"Then what?"

"Are you with me or against me?"

"Raymond! What are you talking about?"

"Where did you change your clothes?"

"What does that matter *now*?"

"Why didn't you come?"

"I don't want to talk about that."

"Were you with him?"

"I don't want to talk about that!"

"What am I to you?"

"Raymond! How can you think about anything else?"

"Because *I can't stop thinking* about something else. Where did he take you?"

"The police will be here any moment. We had better come to an agreement."

"About what?"

"About what I'm going to say."

"What does that matter now?"

"You helped me, now I have to help you."

"Why did you ask me to get rid of him if you loved him?"

"We call *love* things that are *so* different. It's senseless to talk about that."

Now another siren blew stridently. We looked at each other. That was enough to know what was coming.

There was a knock at the door. I went to the bathroom to fetch a towel. I dried my perspiration and called for them to come in. As usual, there were two of them.

"Doctor Papst...," said the one in the grey suit, crossing his arms behind him.

"I know," I interrupted.

"We have to ..."

"I know that too. Spare me the line I've heard in five hundred cops-and-robbers films, officer."

He pointed with his jaw toward the door, and his bald companion stepped aside to make way. Sophie came toward me. For a moment I sensed in her a tight and passionate embrace. But at a breath's distance away, she changed her mind and said to me softly, solemnly:

"You can count on me."

I spontaneously broke out in an ingenuous smile, one which my melancholy diminished. I took one last look at that temple conceived for love's crowning, replete with vain and frivolous objects. Those silk sheets with the hotel emblem embroidered in pink thread, the delicious moisture on the silver champagne pail, the drop of the bleeding heart on the tapestry, and on the bed, like a farewell slap, once more the book by Milosz. I slipped it into my pocket and headed for the door. At the threshold, Sophie's voice stopped me.

"Raymond?"

I spun on my heels and felt my love was intact. Her image again radiated everything that had attracted me to her. Lightness, harmony, warmth, nobility, and skin, once more especially skin.

"My love?"

I thought I saw her lower lip swell with sadness, and I noticed a lipstick smear on her cheek at the moment when she said

to me:
"Nice way to break eggs, don't you think?"

*   *   *

My lawyer, Lawford, placed a hand on my shoulder. I had to get used·to very different dimensions of time. I should make believe I had entered a spaceship that would take me light years away from the petty details and passions of this earth. The only secret for surviving from a week to twenty years in the *cooler*—he used that happy term—was to arm myself with the patience of Job. Any eagerness to get out from behind bars succeeds only in increasing the fretting, transforming time into a morass that, millimeter by millimeter, sucks the life out of you. He offered to bring me a book that had helped some clients who were serving frightful sentences. Something like "Techniques for Evasion in Penal Centers." The title, he said, was crassly ambiguous, but the guards now let it pass into the jails because they knew the sullen author used the term "evasion" in the French sense, that is, as the art of entertaining oneself. I told Lawford I appreciated his offer, but I had so much to think about and I kept myself so passionately busy polishing my unruly obsessions, that I really had no time for his manual. On the other hand, I urgently requested a copy of Braganza's clinical report, x-rays included, so I could evaluate professionally my chances. Besides, if he would be so kind, would he have today's paper sent to me. With a tap on his briefcase the attorney made it understood he had a copy inside.
"But I didn't want to show it to you," he said. "It might spoil your digestion and your mood."
"Spare me the delicacy. Show me the worst you have."
"No way. I'll show you the gentlest."
He unfolded the cover of a tabloid in Italian where there appeared postcard-size photos of Sophie, myself, Braganza, and— the earth trembles!—my legitimate wife Ana. Above them, written in red blood, the following headline: TUTTI SIAMO CORNUTTI. I grabbed the paper with a swipe, crumpled it into a ball, and set it on fire with a match. The guard peevishly came over

and watched the paper burning on the cement floor. My lawyer stepped on it and in a few seconds managed to put it out.

"You have to try to be rational," he pronounced. "A half million copies of this newspaper are sold daily. It's not worth the effort of condemning only one of them to the flames."

*   *   *

Then he opened his attaché case wide and extracted some fifteen books, placing them delicately on my narrow bed.

"And what is this?" I said.

"An idea," he exclaimed, ruffling his enviable alabaster hair. "I thought we might bolster your defense with some literary jurisprudence. Do you follow me?"

"No."

"You ... Don't take this wrong, since it's really for your own good. With your *eccentric* love affair, you are a difficult, though not a totally anomalous case."

"Listen here, Mr. Lawford. When I fell in love from my kidneys to my left parietal lobe, with all its emotional and motor functions, I didn't do it to be interesting but to obey the dictates of my spirit and my flesh."

"I understand, Dr. Papst. I am not accusing you of *sexual* plagiarism." He could not help but smile at this find. "I am trying to persuade you to help me divest your case of the morbid, parodic, and monstrous tone the press wants to give it, a factor that will necessarily exercise a strong influence on public opinion and, to be sure, on the courts. You know what Wilde said about public opinion and England."

"I know Wilde by heart, sir."

"So much the better. What I want you to do is to take a look at these books and compare your experience with these heroes and heroines, to assay their foibles and failings, to recuperate their most human qualities, to *sense* their innocence. I need to present you to the judges as pure as a newborn babe."

"Tell me, Mr. Lawford ... Have you gone to the trouble of procuring this documentation for me yourself?"

He adjusted the knot of his tie. A gesture that showed a certain displeasure at my question.

"Oh, no, Doctor! I am one of those who think books bite. But I have in my office a small battalion of unemployed humanists who write up my briefs using examples taken from literature. I am creating a sort of *fantastic jurisprudence* that has earned me an article in *The Times*."

"Pardon my inquisitiveness, but I am assaulted by a very legitimate concern."

"What's that?"

"Do you win your cases with this method?"

"Sometimes I win, sometimes I lose. No more or less than before I started to use it. But *The Times* named me the most original barrister of the year."

Awash in fate, I glanced at the spines of the texts Lawford had assigned me. They included Nabokov, Benedetti, Goetz, Catullus, Poe, and the Bible.

Excellent literature, to be sure, but clustered about a single theme these noble books served only to perfect my obsessions. Once the human horizon was cleared, I had only the consolation of literature. I began with flights of lyricism and landed on Edgar Allan Poe, whose Annabel Lee I had read with comic singsong as a schoolboy, not paying attention to its contents. At that time I was no older than the heroine, and death was the planet to which everyone traveled sooner or later, but it would never be my fate. Overwhelmed now with knowledge of Poe's biography, which tells how, after being fired for drunkenness from the *Southern Literary Messenger*, he obtained a license in 1836 to marry Virginia Clemm, his thirteen-year-old cousin (how merciful is my savage country toward love's blindness), I weighed every word of his verses until I knew them by heart, my lips whispering to the wind between the bars of my cell. There was no doubt that the poem had not been inspired but rather dictated by the death of Virginia, a victim of tuberculosis in their house at Fordham. It was, I swear, not arrogance but pain that led me to interpret the fourth stanza as part of my own biography:

The angels, not half so happy in Heaven,
Went envying her and me:
Yes! that was the reason (as all men know,
In this kingdom by the sea)
That the wind came out of the cloud, chilling
And killing my Annabel Lee.

My angels, with jaundiced faces, libidinous saliva, twisted horns, disgusting groins, sulfurous forks, were Allan Bracourt, the entrepreneur Forbes, Countess von Mass, the photographers, the hotel doormen, the cab drivers, the thousands of spectators on the international circuit, the millions of TV viewers who consumed Sophie Mass's image. All of them together had driven me to delirium, shackling me with their envy and mutilating my freedom with their snares. Among the countless millions, she had preferred me, and even if she were the most anonymous of tennis players in some club in the provinces, I would have loved her the same. But it was fame that made her appealing, that attracted tragedy to her. The endless circle of fans worked their witchcraft to keep me from Sophie, they stuck pins in dolls, licked the umbilical cords of lactating mothers, bled their wrists so I would stumble and fall, so that a loaded revolver would appear between my fingers just at the wrong moment, so that a pharisee could photograph me naked in her arms. What an army of repulsive seraphim lined the route of my funeral procession!

*   *   *

After excusing himself for not having shown up three days before, as we had agreed, my lawyer said he had spectacular news. He loosened the knot of his tie and, digging through his attaché case, extracted an envelope with which, like a clown, he hit himself in the forehead.

"I don't know what this message says, but I do know what I have to say to you. This is a letter from your victim, Pablo Braganza."

I grabbed it and, with a ceremonious gesture of clairvoyance, placed it over my brow.

"If he writes, he is alive," I philosophized.

"I wasn't able to get x-rays or clinical reports for you because they're guarding them under lock and key. But the patient himself told me in confidence that not only is his life not in danger but he hopes to be released from the hospital next week. He wrote this message in my presence."

I went over to the window and for a minute watched a basketball game between some Hindu and Pakistani prisoners, who shot wildly at a netless hoop. I made the motion of hitting a make-believe ball with an imaginary racket.

"What does the victim's recovery mean for my trial?"

"From the 'perfect crime,' with a death and all, to 'attempted murder,' with the client alive and twitching: ten years less in jail. Congratulations, Dr. Papst."

"And in terms of time spent, how much would that be?"

"In terms of time spent, it means that with a little luck I can get you out in only ten years."

"Ten years! Dr. Lawford, would you be so kind as to find me another attorney?"

"We could try to base your defense on the thesis of your insanity, which strikes everyone as extremely ridiculous" (precisely because all truth is ridiculous, he had the decency to add), "but which has the advantage of allowing for some courtroom theatrics. This always impresses the judges, who would be struggling to convict you of 'premeditated murder with minimally mitigating circumstances.' Let's say, in terms of time spent, seven years. A *bocatto di cardinali!*"

"And what would be the mitigating circumstances?"

"The books I've brought you. You'll look thoroughly batty."

My lips were dry. I ran my tongue over them and thought sadly about the bottles of Dom Perignon confiscated in the prison office.

"Seven years!" I sighed.

"The nymph would be twenty-two and you, fifty-nine. A piece of cake!"

"Not a single word must come out against Sophie!"

"Doctor Papst, you are a hopeless romantic. That kind of behavior ties my hands and feet. A trial with a little hot sauce would spice up the judges' daily routine and would confirm my reputation. The only other alternative is for that letter to contain very good news."

"Such as what?"

"For example, that the young man retracted his complaint."

My cheeks were pounding with blood. I picked up my handkerchief to dry my forehead.

"Owe my freedom to my rival? ... I'd rather commit *hara kiri* than subscribe to that mockery!"

"You're not an easy man to defend. If you insist on moral victories, you're going to be so old when you get out of jail, the only way you'll thrill your loved one will be through the lips."

This ambiguity was worthy of the most circumspect Mexican translator.

"What should I do then?"

"For starters, open the letter."

I broke the seal, and as I did so I saw that a piece of transparent adhesive tape covered the glue. A possible indication that someone had already opened it: the district attorney, the judge, the guard, or my lawyer. I gave Lawford the envelope, granting him a grimace of suspicion, and I plunged into the message.

Papst:

Rat among rats, pirate dung, street corner hitman, shadowy gangster, Yankee gunslinger, purebred cuckold, drooling satyr, castrated carrion eater, mangy pustule, traitorous opportunist, denizen of the sewers! I regret I have yet to be released from the hospital, for I would have liked to shout the foregoing to your face. I never thought your cowardice would come to this: I fired at you with metaphors, and you have fired at me with bullets. You don't know how to lose, ridiculous ignoramus and ass kisser, and you understand nothing but violence, the reason of beasts. But you didn't get me, son-of-a-bitch! Sophie paid me a visit and con-

firmed her love for me. As soon as I get out of this place, we are
going to celebrate a festival in bed and I will see to it that the
mattress springs screech until your eardrums explode.

Your attorney tells me that, because I have survived this
attempted murder, they might reduce your sentence. I want to
assure you that I would have liked to die, just so you could have
rotted in jail. I'll have my lawyers send you away for twenty years.
I'll keep you posted as to developments in my life with Sophie and
I'll supply you with books. Console yourself with literature,
knave, panderer, pimp, whore, cur, vermin, impotent charlatan,
bungler, greenhorn, churl, botcher, asshole, turd, disgusting old
toad.

Your faithful friend and admirer,

Pablo Braganza

I turned around and leapt to grasp hold of the bars, which I
shook as if it were they that were keeping the air from reaching my
lungs. I sensed I was about to faint. I needed oxygen. A cockroach
was walking down the iron bar and was about to climb onto my
hand. I squashed it with my fist and ran to the sink, on the verge of
vomiting.

"You have to get me out of here," I cried to the lawyer.

"We'll do everything possible. Seven, maybe six years."

"No! Right now."

"Doctor. I'm only a lawyer, not the Great Houdini."

*   *   *

The rest of the day and all through the night I devoured the
fantastical-juridical mini-library of Lawford's advisors:

Genesis, for the case of Joseph and Potiphar's wife, where
the good and chaste man winds up in the *cooler* because of the
woman's accusations, with the aggravating factor that in prison he
turns into a shrink and analyses his companions' dreams.

Death in Venice, with the understanding that the
protagonist's tribulations were incomparably more complex than
mine, because unless I've been lying in the preceding pages, I as

Romeo had at least one night of love; not like poor Aschenbach, who had to stew twice before he died: first in his thoughts and second beneath the pestilent sun of the Venetian beach, achieving thereby an immortal German novel but a pretty shitty death.

Then *Tatiana*, the diminutive cellist who via Dvorak and Bach had at the age of thirteen married my colleague Boris Mikhailovich Leventieff, only to die frozen in a windstorm in which she immolated herself according to the logic of Russian nonsense.

And later, in one sitting, *The Truce* by Mario Benedetti, where Laura Avellaneda, who with her youth has given new vigor to the life of the retired Martín Santomé, decides to die without any symptoms or explanation.

And of course *Lolita*, with my cellmate Humbert Humbert, the girl's lover, who was presented to me by Lawford's team so we could distinguish my case from that of a premeditated murder, which is what Humbert Humbert perpetrates against Quayle: he fires a battery of bullets at him, reloads the revolver, has him read a testament, and finally rejects the disgusting ploy of having an accidental homicide blamed on him. Mediocre and conventional though my arguments might be, I am obliged to do more honor to truth than literature, since Nabokov was writing a book and I was living my life: *I may have lost contact with reality for a second or two—oh, nothing of the I-just-blacked-out sort that your common criminal enacts; on the contrary, I want to stress the fact that I was responsible for every shed drop of his bubbleblood*, which is to say that he, as a tragic figure, assumed complete responsibility for every drop of Clare Quilty's alcoholic blood that he spilled, whereas I, as a parodic postmodern antihero, had to repeat the scripted blackout of the grade "B" films that Nabokov had already ironized *avant la lettre*.

Toward dawn I felt cramps in my stomach, as if rather than having read them I had eaten hundreds of pages of those books. It was hot and I had a fever. All things considered, my fate was somewhat less miserable than that of the gallery of heroes with which I had tormented myself. In the majority of cases the heroine died at the hands of the jealous lover, in the other main variant the assassin was the lover's rival, and in still other texts the authors dispatched the girl to heaven with an unforeseen illness (Poe, Goetz, Benedetti). In plain talk, my situation was the stuff of a Harlequin romance compared to that of those ladies and gentlemen: my opponent, perforated and all, was alive and ready to massacre mattresses; my love, notwithstanding her defeat at Wimbledon, had at fifteen years of age no reason to declare an end to her career, and Raymond Papst had lost nothing more than his wife, his practice, his home, his inheritance, his Oldsmobile limousine, his beloved, his prestige, and his freedom. In all, nothing serious. Encouraged by these reflections, I decided to give Mr. Braganza a piece of my mind, and in order to avoid descending to the level of his exalted epistolary style, I settled on representing myself via Catullus's poem Number Thirty-Seven:

> *puella nam mi, quae meo sinu fugit,*
> amata tantum quantum amabitur nulla,
> pro qua mihi sunt magna bella pugnata,
> consedit istic, hanc boni beatique
> omnes amatis, et quidem, quod indignum est,
> omnes pusilli et semitarii moechi;
> tu praeter omnes une de capillatis,
> cuniculosae Celtibariae fili,
> Egnati, opaca quem bonum facit barba
> *et dens Hibera defricatus urina.*

Which is to say:

> So my girl, who fled from my arms,
> Who was more beloved than anyone
> Can be loved,
> The one for whom I undertook great battles,
> Fornicates here. And all you gentle noblemen
> Take her, along with the depraved
> Prostibulary rabble.
> Among them *you*, with your long mane,
> A native of Spain, the country of rabbits,

Who brags of his trim beard
And rinses his teeth in urine.

The drawbacks to sending these verses were numerous, but
my fever, my rancor, and my asphyxiation did not give me wise
counsel.

When they brought breakfast, I handed the message to the
guard along with five pounds, three for him and two so it could be
sent special delivery. I had a cup of coffee with milk and made
ready to sleep, bubbling with impatience. I wanted the message to
reach Braganza's hands before I fell asleep. I imagined him with
his snout smashed, vomiting bile through the corners of his lips.
Just at that moment I heard the call of a neighbor's eccentric
rooster, and five minutes later the birds' din was in full swing.
Amidst that concert I drifted off into slumber, providing a comfortable nest for my nightmares.

*   *   *

The guard returned with three men dressed in white, two of
whom were complacently chewing gum, while the third, redolent
with authority, immediately impressed me as a psychiatrist. As
soon as they opened the cell door he extended his hand to me and
shook mine very cordially. Afterwards he glanced at the books and
then pushed them aside so he could sit on the corner of my damp
bed.

He flipped indifferently through the complete poems of
Poe and then rubbed his chin. For a while he stared at my bare feet,
and only at that instant did I realize that I was naked, wrapped in
the sheet, just as in the nightmare. I touched my cheek and felt the
rough growth of my beard. What an ideal choreography for a
psychiatrist. He raised his eyes and smiled at me:

"So, another night jousting with windmills, my lord Don
Quixote."

The smile with which I had responded to his smile came
undone on me. I tensed my facial muscles, and in a rage I grabbed
the thermometer from the guard's hand.

"I am burning up with fever, Doctor. I need an aspirin, not an asylum."

He gestured for me to put the instrument in my mouth, which I did aggressively. He opened the Bible toward the middle of the volume and tarried a minute among the central pages. Then he came toward me and extracted the thermometer with a dry pull, like one removing a thorn.

"Forty degrees centigrade, my colleague. How did you manage to catch such a fever?"

"I didn't do anything. It just came."

"Since I specialize in illnesses of the mind, which are somewhat more intangible than yours, allow me to ask you for a self-diagnosis."

"A cold."

"How did it *come*?"

Even inside that pressure cooker I suffered flashes of lucidity. By underscoring the verb *to come*, the psychiatrist was differentiating it from more active verbs, like *to do*. That is, he was investigating whether I had somehow concocted the fever. His motives would reveal themselves shortly.

"I was sweating while I slept. Unconsciously I threw off the cover. The sweat cooled on me. Grippe."

"So you want to spend a while in the infirmary, Raymond."

One had to notice the familiar use of the first name linked with the word "infirmary." Suddenly I imagined it to be an orgiastic place, at any rate better than this pigsty where the only entertainment was my hallucinations. So that was the difference between *to do* and *to come*: the infirmary.

"Of course, my boy. I'm dying for a few days of revelry."

"Fine. And as soon as that temperature returns to normal, let's talk about the thingies that go through your headie at night."

"Whatever you wish, my boy. What's your name?"

"Donald Ray, Junior. My friends call me *Duckie*."

In a jiffy we made a bundle of my toilet articles, pajamas, and a couple of shirts, but when I was about to grab my books, the psychiatrist stopped me.

"The picnic will be without between-meal snacks. In order

to see where the problem lies, we have to remove all the phantasms from your grey matter. So leave all that stuff in the cell."

"Anything you say, my boy."

As we were walking down the stairs, with the two robust guards maintaining a sporting silence, Doctor Ray, Junior squeezed my elbow and said to me in confidence:

"Are you playing the loonie so they declare you innocent, or are you really *loco*?"

I gave him a cordial slap on his erudite back.

"*Loco*, Duckie! Completely and absolutely *loco*!"

$$* \quad * \quad *$$

Had my life's objective changed?

No.

What did I want?

Sophie!

Hunger for Sophie, thirst for Sophie, heat and heaven of Sophie, navel of Sophie, fleshy round springlike nipple of Sophie at the center of my destiny! Had conditions changed since the last time I took stock?

No, sir.

No word of her.

Did this mean she didn't love me any more? Probably, but not for certain. Having defined my objective, my goal now was to escape from jail in order to accomplish it. Doctor Raymond Papst, after seven or ten years in jail, would be the shadow of a man, and although sweet Sophie might visit me once a year during her tournaments in London, bringing me poems and chocolates, it was clear that those who prophesied the worst for me did not do so to distress me but rather to move me to adopt a realistic outlook.

Ergo, I had to go into my Birdman of Alcatraz act. Split, disappear, blow the joint, make myself scarce, fly the coop, make a break for it, according to the expressions I learned from my fellow captives in the clink.

After breakfast, which I voraciously consumed under the stimulus of these new plans, the nurse told me that in a matter of a half hour Dr. Ray, Junior would visit me to talk at length about my case. I told her I was glad, and I turned to the job of completing my scheme. I was immersed in that when I heard a knock at my door. This courtesy is unknown in jail, where even the lowliest attendant is likely to kick down your door like some John Wayne. To respond in kind to that show of refinement, I did not shout *come in* but went to the door and opened it gently.

It was Sophie Mass in person. She wore a tailored grey suit and had had the delirious inspiration to sport on her little head a garnet-colored felt hat with a veil of the same color that covered her eyes, in the style of the forties. This imposing choreography was supported by two pointy heels that raised her five centimeters over her actual height, from which rose stockings whose mesh continued in sibyline fashion a good way up her thighs. The tailored skirt did not reach down to her knees, ending with a slit that almost revealed the most secret parts of her flesh.

In the doorway itself she stood tall and planted a kiss on my cheek. I took her cheekbones in my hands and gazed at her, knowing that no kiss could exhaust all the love and desire of that instant.

I took one of Sophie's hands; after putting aside the pages of my febrile notes, I had her sit in the only chair while I sat on the edge of my bed without letting go of her hand.

"You have so much to tell me," I said to her.

"There will be plenty of time for that! For now, listen carefully. This weekend is the beginning of the tournament in Los Angeles, so I have to leave on Friday. It may be a long time before we see each other again."

"Will you write to me?"

The blink of her eyes hit me like a punch. She extracted from her purse a map of London, folded it to the segment that included the jail, and she put her finger on a cross at the edge of a park.

"Raymond, I'm not into that sappy scene of writing letters. You helped me, and now I'm helping you."

"How?"

"I've planned your jailbreak."

I squelched an incredulous smile that threatened to spread across my face and instead looked attentively at the map.

"When?"

"Tomorrow."

My sigh lifted the corner of the map. Sophie began to trace with a fingernail the way from the jail to the Palace of Justice. She stopped at the entrance to the park.

"They'll be taking you to your first interrogation session at eight o'clock. It's supposed to be a confrontation with Braganza. In the police car only one guard will be with you. At the spot marked with this cross, a cab is going to block the road. There will be a fuss. That is the moment when you get out of the car and escape down the Metro stairs."

The designated point was the corner of Grosvenor Place and Halkin Street, across from the gardens of Buckingham Palace. And the Metro station she proposed was Hyde Park, but taking the Pembroke entrance.

"And you?" I asked.

"I'll be praying everything turns out all right."

"Where?"

"Nearby."

"Listen, little one. It's bad enough one of us is in jail. I know this is a tremendous line to feed you, but I gladly bear this burden for love. I don't want you to risk your freedom for me."

"As far as the law is concerned, I'm a minor. If they catch me, they can box my ears, but they won't throw me in jail."

"Let's suppose everything works out according to your plans. How does our life go on?"

"For a while we don't see each other. And then you look me up."

"And what about Braganza?"

"I'm yours alone."

Sophie grew serious. She took a piece of paper from her purse and covered the map of London, smoothing it with her palms. She had spoken hastily, and now she halted in mid-gesture as if we had all the time in the world. After a minute she removed the hat from her head and placed it on her knees, and only then did she give me the stern look of a country schoolmarm.

Then she stood up and handed me the hat so I could put it on her. I grabbed her chin and lifted it violently.

"Answer my question," I said, biting the words. "I need the truth. I desperately need the truth. What happens to Braganza?"

She very tamely placed a hand on mine and then bent her neck so our hands stayed together on her shoulder.

"Good luck, Raymond," she whispered before dissolving through the bars and fading into the London sky, where an imminent storm brewed.

*   *   *

I poured myself a few shots with the psychiatrist, and I asked him what would happen if I tried to escape.

"Nothing, my good man," he told me. "They fill out a form certifying you flew the coop, they stamp it and send it to Scotland yard. They call your friends and relatives and ask for you. If they don't find you at home, they file it, old man."

"That simple."

"With you, yes, because you're small fry. Just think, you shot the guy at point-blank range and he's still walking around alive and well, disputing the tennis star with you. Everyone takes you for a pussycat, kid."

"So I could stand up, walk out of here, and you wouldn't do anything."

"It wouldn't affect me in the slightest. You would have to cross the patio, where they hunt you down with the reflectors, they shout for you to halt, and if you don't obey they fire a couple of volleys into the air. If all goes well you make it to the exit, and there you have to have figured out the code with which to enter the computer room, and once in the computer room, you have to know the number to press in order to open the main door. If you pass that last barrier, you still have to contend with the guards in the street, who do have the order to shoot at the body. If you want some advice from a colleague, don't try it. The chances of their getting you were published a couple of weeks ago in the prison annual. The boys have a macabre sense of humor. They call their magazine *Flight*."

"How many successful escapes have there been?"

"None. From here, it's impossible."

I gestured for him to come near and I whispered near his hairy earlobe.

"Can I trust you as a friend and colleague?"

"Naturally."

"You won't give me away if I tell you something?"

"I swear it."

I looked at him with my eyes on fire.

"Sophie paid me a visit."

I was proud of the impact this information had on Donald. He rubbed his chin and brought his face close to mine, lowering the volume.

"She paid you a visit in jail?"

"That's right."

"And how did she get in?"

"I didn't see her enter, but I did see her leave, so I presume she entered as she left."

"How?"

"You're not going to believe me: she evaporated."

With this good news, Donald grew intensely interested.

"Do you mean to tell me she disappeared into thin air?"

"Exactly."

"How odd! And you don't think it was a dream?"

"She came to plan my escape. It'll happen tomorrow when they transfer me from the jail to the courthouse. Sophie's organized everything. Do you think she'll go through with it?"

"If your chickie has your escape planned, if I were you I'd do everything possible to blow this place. With the sentence they'll give you, while you're in the cooler her suitors will eat her up, bones and all."

"Between colleagues," I said in a solemn tone, "how much time do you think they'll give me?"

"Seven."

"But that's the same thing my lawyer promises me!"

"In London they're strict about bearing firearms."

"As a foreigner, I had no way of knowing the legislation!"

"That's why it would be seven and not ten." A wave of pallor must have washed over me, for he raised his glass proposing a toast. "Cheer up, my man, for here we're having a grand time."

We clinked glasses and I made a note to myself to send him a postcard the following week, thanking him for his objective input.

"Tomorrow is the big day," he added. "They'll come and get you in a white car. A great white car."

*   *   *

When they came to pick me up early the next day, the guards found Dr. Raymond Papst dressed in formal attire. A suit with a French cut impeccably ironed by the nurse, a silk tie with a somewhat ostentatious tie bar, a shirt stiff with starch topped off with millionaire cufflinks, and a half pound of styling gel so not one hair was out of place. I wanted to give the guard who accompanied me in the car the impression that, rather than guard me, his mission was to protect the Minister of Foreign Affairs against some terrorist attack.

Under normal circumstances I would not have gone to such sartorial extremes, but a good suit and my Bostonian prickliness would surely have some effect on a goon whose chief claim to fame consisted of spitting at the dart game on the walls of his pub. I was therefore not concerned about having spent those extra pounds, which I would need so dearly, for the nurse's extracurricular services.

My colleague Ray, Jr. authorized the issuing of the tie, signing in his own hand that there was no risk of my hanging myself. A look at the hallway mirror revealed to me the desired image, and I sighed with satisfaction. I tried to ice the cake with the following gambit: when the ambulance arrived I did not open the door, but rather imperiously waited for the guard to do it for me. My teeth chattered when he bellowed at me with his Neanderthal voice:

"Move your ass, pretty boy, before I kick it in for you."

Now I knew what the stakes were. I had not the slightest
doubt that the gunman would have no second thoughts about
proffering me a bullet to the temples if I gave a suspect twitch. To
certify this impression, he sank down in the rear seat of the car and
with a sour expression rested his hairy paw over his revolver
holster. Up front sat two armed nurses as well. According to
Sophie's calculations, we would reach the ambush point in about
fifteen minutes, more than enough time for me to come to terms
with my life.

Crime has its own logic and a giddiness inherent to it. One
thing leads to the next. A little while ago I was tortured, for fear
of reprisals, by the thought of kissing the girl I loved. And now that
I had shot someone—now that I was outside the law—I was going
to ruin my chances for a benign sentence by attempting a spectacular escape that would leave my attorney livid. With a smile, I
wondered where the road less taken would lead me. I felt a tickling
in my heart. I was really filled with enthusiasm for my nonsense.
The idea that the next step was to fight for Sophie's love struck me
as tortuous but still infinitely more attractive than going back to
foisting pills on my elderly Berliner patients.

The traffic in London at that hour of the morning moves at
a snail's pace, so I had time also to cast a sympathetic glance at all
those beings caught up in their vacuous routines. One had to endow
life with meaning. I corrected that adolescent maxim: one had to
endow life *with an act* that shed light on those tunnels where we
engulf ourselves.

Seeing those thousands of people obsessed with arriving
punctually at their vapid appointments, I understood that although
my life, like theirs, lacked sense, I was about to commit *the* act, no
matter how fleeting it might be nor how uncertain its outcome. At
Kensington Road I defined in Baudelairian terms my stance with
respect to existence. They all wanted the emotion of the danger,
but without risking so much as a plug nickel, or even the clipping
from their pinky fingernail. To this point, convinced of the truth
of the maxim that discretion is the better part of valor, I have been
careful with my language. But now, on the verge of finishing my
tale, I am going to indulge myself in an obscenity that comes from

the heart: "Take your world and shove it up your ass." I, Doctor Raymond Papst, was made of flesh and blood and dreams, and I was going to perpetrate *my act.*

The map I had memorized indicated we would reach the crossroad of Grosvenor Place and Halkin in a couple of minutes. It was a radiant day. The display windows in the stores returned a hundredfold the rays of the morning sun, filling the air with nervous particles. I felt my cheek burning when I pressed it against the car window. Then I touched the door handle. In a few seconds I would have to depress it, open the door, and start to run. The lock was set. I drummed on it with my fingers, and with a distracted air I lifted it without drawing the clumsy guard's attention. At that moment a cab crossed violently from the left and the driver of our car slammed on the brakes so abruptly that all of us were thrown forward. The guard's door was opened from outside. There was Sophie Mass.

I would have expected a battalion of masked men from the IRA, Cardiff gunslingers with nylon stockings distorting their faces, shoeshine boys from Liverpool, and teenage hooligans with spiked hairdos, thugs from New York flown to London on the Concorde, meticulous Chinamen with crescent knives at their nervous phalanges, lofty Zulus with bloodshot eyes and lances scraping the clouds, Mexican *pistoleros* with belts of ammunition across their chest and their faces hidden in the shadow of their *sombreros*, Italian *mafiosi* with bare chests and little medallions with a cross above the point of their menacing knives, a battalion of pygmies that would nip at the guard's heels and gnaw at the car's tires till they were worn out, Japanese *kamikazes* tossing their knives into the air like a festival of streamers, any person or group, battalion, contingent, race, band, miscreation of the human species, but *never, never ever* did I expect to see participate in this criminal operation Sophie Mass in person.

At the very instant when the girl had opened the door, the guard, with the reflexes of a tiger, pulled his revolver from his holster. The barrel was pointing straight at Sophie's forehead, and a terrified shout rose from the depths of my soul. The premonition of death, induced by all the agonistic heroines of my lettered jailhouse *soirées*, had me imagine in a flash the death of my angel, her forehead splintered by that beast's bullet, her vigorous blood spilled on the pavement in front of Buckingham Palace. Her shining eyes and her willful jaw gestured, commanding me to leap from the car and flee. The driver who had stopped us was standing beside his vehicle, watching my inaction in disbelief, not understanding that Sophie's appearance had petrified me. I will never know if that delay was a blessing or a curse. I only remember that the guard brutally slammed his door shut and depressed the lock button. I remember that the driver threw the car into reverse and in a quick maneuver avoided the taxi that was blocking him. I evoke the image of Sophie, her arms open, her face filled with incomprehension, astonished upon seeing that I was not running away.

I, who was inclined to resort to the rowdiest heroism, felt I was sinking in a swamp of cowardice. It's for her that I did it, I thought. It was to avoid her death that I did not flee. Only an act of renunciation, of fervent sacrifice, had kept the guard from pulling the trigger. Perhaps everything could have or ought to have happened in some other way. Perhaps, upon running toward the Hyde Park Metro the watchman would have fired his bullets at the base of my skull and my blood of a tame lamb—I can find no other noun or adjective with which to despise myself—would have brought my story and my sorrow to an end. My altruism and my felony wanted me to live. In the ambulance, I could not keep from crying for Sophie, but especially for myself, a self-pity I confess, repugnant though it may be to me.

The guard jammed his revolver into the holster and fraternally jabbed me with his elbow:

"Don't cry like a faggot, man," he said.

"But you could have killed Sophie," I yelled at him.

"What Sophie?" asked the brute, scratching his head.

I didn't answer him. In order to keep some people from existing you have to ignore them.

*   *   *

I abbreviate the rest, since almost all of it reeks of medioc-
rity. The barrister and the psychiatrist collaborated wonderfully,
and in a legal brief that will not make juridical history and about
which there was not so much as a paragraph in the press, they
convinced a sleepy tribunal of my insanity. They had me commit-
ted to this asylum, but Donald is certain they'll release me in a
couple of years. Sophie won the tournament in Los Angeles, but
later she lost a lackluster championship in Melbourne, another
fifth-rate one in Montreal, and she was finalist—but finally lost—
in the U.S. Open in New York. The papers reported with abundant
graphics on her sweet-sixteen party in Majorca. In the pictures she
is shown surrounded by ladies and gentlemen with suntanned
faces—yachting fanciers with sun-bleached hair and frivolously
light-colored clothes. Among them on one occasion, with a
tormented face and a gaze fixed straight at the camera lens, appears
Pablo Braganza. They delayed in writing me. Only at Christmas
time did I have word from Sophie. On the twenty-fourth of
December the guard brought me a package wrapped in festive gold
paper, sent from St. Louis, Missouri, containing the racket with
which she had won a tournament somewhere in the Ozarks. A card
was attached that read: "Stay in shape. Love, Sophie."
    Braganza, for his part, made his statement by means of a
photo that had the charm of images captured by a box camera in a
provincial plaza. He radiated the same smile I remember on Burt
Lancaster in "The Rainmaker," with one arm around Sophie's
shoulder and her little head resting on his neck. The setting could
have been Spanish or Portuguese. On the back of the snapshot, in
the boy's broad handwriting, there was a delicate dedication:
    "Thinking of you always, Sophie and Pablo."

                    *   *   *

    Ana made her presence felt toward the end of the year with
a little box of champagne for New Year's Eve. It was a half-dozen
bottles of melancholy Pommery, which I consumed at one sitting
in the company of the guard on the night shift and two identical

twins, manic-depressives transferred from the psychiatric ward at Aberdeen.   On the attached postcard she informed me that Mollenhauer, after a jazz concert at the Philharmonic, had *formally* asked for her hand in matrimony. *Verbatim* from Ana: "I turned him down."

Two parting notes.   First, an item of an athletic nature. After the patients leave the basketball court, I go down there dressed in impeccable white, and in an absurd impersonation of a tennis match with a phantasm, I use Sophie's Christmas racket to hit balls against the wall. This pleasure costs me a bribe of sixty pounds per month, not to mention the razzing from all the loonies, who enviously throw apple cores and spit at me from behind the bars of their cells. I follow Sophie's orders and religiously keep myself fit by defeating myself, one hour a day, rain or shine.

And finally, these days there is a popular a song called "Tiebreak" that I hum from morning till night and that, inspired by my twilight groundstrokes, the inmates sometimes intone as well. I empathetically transcribe below one of the stanzas:

> *"It was so much fun to give it a whirl,*
> To enjoy the pleasure of a hidden light,
> But now we are in the eye of the storm:
> *Tiebreak."*

End